DON'T EVEN THINK ABOUT IT!

DON'T EVEN THINK ABOUT IT!

101 Dangerous Things NOT To Do
Before You Grow Old

Richard Wilson

PORTICO

First published in the United Kingdom in 2009 by
Portico Books
10 Southcombe Street
London
W14 0RA

An imprint of Anova Books Company Ltd

ISBN 9781906032746

A CIP catalogue record for this book is available from the British
Library.

10 9 8 7 6 5 4 3 2 1

Printed and bound by CPI Mackays, Chatham ME5 8TD

This book can be ordered direct from the publisher at
www.anovabooks.com

Contents

Introduction

Chapter One: *Home-made Fun*

Chapter Two: *Wholesome Entertainment*

Chapter Three:
Old-fashioned Adventure

Chapter Four: *Proper Holidays*

Chapter Five: *Useful Knowledge*

Set the foot down with distrust on the crust of the world – it is thin.
Edna St Vincent Millay
(What do you mean 'who?')

Introduction

We all like to think our childhood was brilliant, don't we? Not only was everything supposed to be better when we were kids, we apparently had more fun than the present generation of unfortunates; our games were better, we were cleverer, more creative and imaginative, and we didn't spend all day stuck in front of a screen.

Well, this book says: hold on a minute. The 60s and 70s were nothing like the halcyon days people say they were and most of what passed for fun was actually quite rubbish.

There's nothing more boring than being told you should have been around in the 60s, or that the 70s were the best decade ever. The Baby Boomers had plenty of fun mocking their parents for going on about The War but at least the refrain then was 'You were lucky not to live through that!' Now it's 'Ah, but in the 70s we had *real* fun.'

We hear a lot about how unhappy British children are these days (the unhappiest in Europe, supposedly?!). They don't go

1

anywhere or do anything interesting; they're slaves to technology and computers, their exams are too easy, they don't know proper stuff, they don't explore or take risks; they eat too many crisps and can't spell.

Probably none of this is true. Those who control the media just think it is, because they aren't kids any more and are slightly jealous of the people who are. Jealous of their phones, their YouTube, their Facebook, their Wikipedia, their Google, their iPods, their friends, their height and probably their straight teeth.

If Nostalgia literally means a 'painful longing for things past', thn the greatest agony is reserved for lost childhood. The things we did as kids, whether they were dangerous, crap or just boring, are the things we weep over as our own children take our place in the playground.

And now the cries of pain have found a new outlet – the Nostalgia Activity book. A few years ago *The Dangerous Book For Boys* was published, full of super ideas to help boys have 'dangerous' fun, like tying reef knots in curtain cord, making bows and arrows from bulrushes and setting fire to pets with a magnifying glass.

Within weeks dozens of copycat books appeared with titles like *The Dad's Book of Dad's Stuff, The Boy's Book of Harmless Explosions,* and *When I Was A Lad All We Did Was Whittle Wood.*

Apart from trying to climb aboard a very tasty gravy train (made with beef dripping ... granules), these books were all preaching the same message: that we should return to the Old Days when everyone had proper fun; to a time when everything was rosy in the garden of England and we all had exciting adventures on seemingly endless afternoons, helping the police apprehend some burly men who'd been stealing postal orders.

Nowadays, of course, it would be obese men committing benefit fraud, but we can't turn back the clock by writing invisible-ink messages and making a pinhole camera. Skimming stones won't stop knife crime. No amount of pointless but greatly cherished pastimes from our childhood will change modern society.

In fact, we should face up to the fact that the world is only made *more* dangerous by people making their own tinderboxes and Bunsen burners and home-made flame-throwers and careering down hills in soapbox carts.

But this is the era those books with titles like *Wizard Wheezes in Wigwams* and *Family Fun With Pater and Mater* would like to take us back to. They are pining for a 'land of lost content', where we were all supposedly happy and secure, whereas in fact grizzly death and disfigurement were as common as rickets.

Children of the 60s and 70s will often say: 'We were put out to play by our mums and told to just go off for the day and not come back until tea-time.' That's true, but was this for our own self-improvement and good health? No – it was because there was nothing to occupy us at home. No 24-hour TV, no MSN and no PlayStation. If we'd have had those things to keep us quiet for two hours do you think our parents would have been so keen to kick us out?

The assumption is that, in the 50s, 60s and 70s, when everyone was supposed to have had a proper childhood, society in general had devised a programme of activities and parental practices especially designed to bring the best out of kids. What bollocks, of course they didn't! Mothers used to leave babies in prams at the bottom of the garden, not because the fresh air was good for them, but so that they couldn't be heard screaming their heads off (or choking or being suffocated by the neighbour's cat).

You see, the world was a pretty dangerous place in the Old Days: there were abandoned fridges on rubbish tips that kids could climb into and get locked inside; there were unexploded bombs and unsafe building sites; there were teddy boys, bikers, mods and rockers; there were plenty of paedos (on your street for all you knew because there was no Register); there were cars with angular bumpers to guarantee fatal accidents, and no Pelican crossings. And the toys we had were pretty useless and the games we made up were there purely to pass the time. Where's the great imagination in a game of Hide and Seek or Bulldog? Kids still play these games today, of course, but only for about five minutes when the sun's out and only until they think of something better to do.

If every kid *had* possessed a nice camera phone in the 1950s we'd have a brilliant archive on YouTube of scabby-kneed kids blowing themselves up with unexploded Jerry munitions, falling into flooded bomb-craters, cracking their heads on the concrete under the swings and flying kites into overhead power lines. It took decades of Public Information Films and – yes, say it! – Health and Safety Regulations to reduce the astronomical death rates from kids sticking plastic bags on their heads and swallowing bottles of aspirin.

'But you can't wrap your kids in cotton wool, you know.'

Why not? It sounds brilliant, doesn't it? Wrapped in cotton wool – what a wonderful way to treat a child! I'd love to be wrapped in cotton wool right now, wouldn't you?

Of course, no one should begrudge anyone of forty-five and

over their memories of a make-do-and-mend childhood, tree-top hideouts, pea-shooters and secret signs. And clearly books such as *What Dads Should Teach Their Children* and *Wooden Toys To Poke Pater With* are as much nostalgia for the Old Man as something to pass on to his kids. But to present them seriously as a way to mould and shape a 21st-century child into what he ought to be is as futile and annoying as a modern-day politician apologising for the dubious morality of his ancestors.

So you will not find anywhere in this book suggestions for making your own crossbow out of a deckchair or a grappling-hook out of a coat-hanger or even your own maracas out of dried peas. No, its message is: Don't Even Think About doing any of it – you're better off not playing outside at all. Stay indoors where responsible people can see you. Watch TV, play video games and have some harmless fun.

Are we too cautious, too reliant on mobiles and computers and too obsessed with Health and Safety? Yes, and so we should be! Really, computers and mobile phones *are* brilliant, Health and Safety *has* done great things for us and in a world as dangerous as this, caution is the only sensible option.

Don't Go Outside

To be honest, everyone, especially children, would be a lot safer if they stayed indoors. Even going to school is an extremely risky activity which is best avoided, and don't even think about walking it.

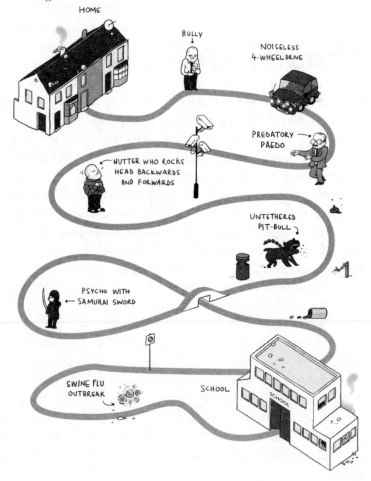

Chapter One
Home-made Fun

The Proper Childhood Police – people who want children to amuse themselves with wooden toys and penknives instead of PlayStations and Wii's – think there's a virtue in making your own stuff to play with. These people seem to have forgotten all those Monty Python sketches about the futility of assembling *Blue Peter*-style contraptions out of sticky-backed plastic and squeezy-bottles. In fact, they would like to turn the clock back even further to the days when the hoop and stick were considered hi-tec and 'Made in Hong Kong' was shorthand for 'work of the devil'.

But we all know that wooden toys had their limitations – no whirring sound effects, no flashing guns, no lights or mechanical motion – and the stuff we made ourselves was basically useless. I used to pretend a bent stick was a gun and it was crap. I longed for a cap-gun or a beautiful plastic ray-gun that whirred and sparked like a futuristic angle-grinder.

Here are some ideas for home-made fun to have with your kids that are guaranteed to disappoint …

Make a Bow and Arrow

Yes, go on, sharpen a stick with a knife and ping it at your mates – what could possibly go wrong?

There's a reason why the arrows children play with tend to have suckers on them now; actually two reasons.

1. It's fun.
2. Blinding is less likely.

I think the phrase 'You'll have someone's eye out with that' actually originated around the time kids were having someone's eye out with a home-made bow and arrow.

If you're a *Sopranos* fan you'll remember how coke-addled psycho, Ralph Cifaretto, is devastated when his son Justin gets an arrow in the chest playing a harmless game of *Lord of the Rings*. Now if mad Ralph, who beat several people to death with his bare hands, can be brought to his knees by a home-made bow and arrow, we should take heed of the lesson to be learned.

Make Your Own Battery

Believe it or not, you *can* make your own battery. It involves, somewhat laboriously, stacking loads of coins interleaved with vinegar-soaked blotting paper, which will generate enough juice to power a tiny torch battery. OK, we are facing ever-increasing energy shortages, and many everyday electrical gizmos require less current than a torch battery. But they will not accommodate a foot-long stack of vinegary 2p coins. If anyone out there can make a home-made battery (as described in the *Dangerous Book For Boys*) fit inside a TV remote I will give you my house, car and a million pounds[1].

I suppose it is educational to know the principles on which a battery works, but they're not exactly scarce, are they? There's no urgent appeal for batteries in Africa. Plus – just because something can be made at home doesn't mean it should be. I've never tasted a home-made curry that was a patch on the local takeaway or even my local ASDA and let's face it, you wouldn't try to make your own shoes, would you? Well, would you?

I actually made my own kitchen once – I did, I got all the bits from Ikea and Wickes, screwed it all together, sawed up some other bits that didn't fit properly and put the handles on and everything. I now know how a fitted kitchen is actually fitted, but my worktop is so far out of true that Oxo cubes roll down it.

Anyway …

[1] I won't, of course.

9

Make a Cart out of Pram Wheels

Some people would have you believe that in 'the good old days' you couldn't move for kids shrieking with laughter as they hurtled down hills approaching Mach 2 in their home-made carts. Actually, the only people I can ever remember doing this were Bully Beef and Chips in the *Dandy*, who normally ended up shooting out of frame accompanied by 'CRASH', 'YULK' and 'YAROO' sounds, eventually emerging in the final panel with huge bumps and massive criss-crossed sticking plasters.

When I was much older, I gained a more detailed knowledge of the injuries that can be caused by travelling downhill too fast…

My dad was a colliery manager in the days when everyone still burned coal in their houses (younger readers may need to look some of these words up) and he managed to get me a summer job working at the head of a new drift mine that had been driven down to the coal face. Drift mines

were long steep tunnels which came into the coal seam at an angle, rather than a vertical shaft. Pretty boring, right? Well, to liven up the two-mile journey down, many of the miners made their own skateboards and carts out of bits of wood and castors, so they could whiz down to the coal face more quickly, start digging out coal earlier and earn more on their productivity deals. Some brave lads even tried sitting on sacks and using the conveyor belt like some giant helter-skelter.

Now, all these methods were quicker than walking, true enough, but the problem they all had after building up speeds of, say, twenty miles an hour, was stopping. Many used the crude but effective method of slamming into solid rock or the coal-cutting machinery at the bottom. This obviously had its consequences; my job then was to fill in the accident reports so that the injured coal surfers didn't give the health and safety game away (yes, people thought about that even then). So a sample accident report might say:

Nature of injury: Fractured eye-socket, broken fingers, dislocated knee.
Cause of Accident: Fell over

It seems to me that the fundamental problem with any home-made, wheel-based transportation is that you need a slope for it to work. And something to stop you that isn't a wall. Look, if the thrill of self-propulsion excites you so much, why don't you just buy a bike?

• • • • • • • • • • • •

Conkers

• •

Yes, OK, I accept that a conker is a natural thing which you don't literally 'make', but it takes a lot of man-hours to turn the raw material of the horse chestnut into a potential fiver, sixer, tenner or, if you are a pathological liar like most children, a ninety-niner[1].

Finding a horse-chestnut tree that is not diseased is tricky in itself. If you do stumble across one you'll probably find nothing but a carpet of empty shells turning brown and yucky at the bottom. So you'll probably have to whack at the higher branches with sticks or climb up and shake it to get a meagre haul of their lovely shiny nuts. Then, depending whose recipe you're following, you have to bake, soak, pickle in vinegar, blanch, par-boil, sauté, flambé or pan-fry your conker until it's become as hard as rock, or more likely shrunk, fallen to bits and generally deflated. Two days later when the nut has 'rested', you can attempt to drill a hole in it ready for the knotted shoelace (if they still make shoelaces). The drilling of the hole is perhaps the most dangerous part of the conker-making process. Many times my dad's bradawl slipped off the top of the conker and pierced the palm of the hand I was holding it in. You just cannot get a decent enough grip on a small round rock-hard nut to put a

---

[1] For the uninitiated, a winning conker earns the rank of the number of other conkers it has beaten in a contest, even inheriting all the points of a conquered conker, so if a virgin conker beats a fiver, for example, it immediately becomes a sixer. If Gordon Brown was a conker he would be a None-er.

proper hole in it. I would usually give up at this point, either to put all my conkers in a bag to sell at school or to go down to casualty to have the wound in my hand stitched.

But just suppose you do actually get to the final stage – the conker is drilled, the lace is knotted and threaded through, your oak-smoked char-grilled conker (with a herb-crust) is dangling confidently between you and Bernard O'Neil as he readies his own weapon to strike the first blow. You are waiting to survive the first impact so that you can smash Bernard O'Neil's conker to smithereens. He raises, he swings and crack! His aim is hopeless and he brings the full force of the swinging conker to bear on the knuckles of your holding-hand. You scream and drop your conker on the ground, swearing at Bernard O'Neil and kicking your own conker away in a tizzy. A teacher appears, everyone's conkers are confiscated and you get the blame for crying out.

There was a notorious incident recently in which a head-teacher was roundly condemned by the tabloids for banning conkers at his school unless the children wore safety goggles to protect them from flying conker shrapnel. What an idiot! Everyone knows 99 per cent of conker injuries are as I've described – knuckle and finger damage from poorly aimed conkers.

Conkers can bring pain, misery and unhappiness in other ways. The house we lived in as children had the only horse-chestnut tree for about thirty miles and the local primary school teacher helpfully brought thirty kids along one day to point it out to them. Pretty soon, finding an urchin scaling the garden wall and shinning up the tree became a daily occurrence. In a way I take my hat off to them because the garden wall was six feet high and topped with broken glass and barbed wire. Look, this was a mining village and my dad was colliery manager – we weren't popular. Anyway, that year my brothers and I spent more time firing air pistols at local kids than we did playing conkers. It did deter the conker thieves but some of the kids ended up with painful bruises and the Wilson boys received cautions from the police. I doubt whether everyone reading this has shared all of my experiences with conkers, but I think I have gone some way to proving that there is no such thing as harmless fun.

Build Your Own Den

What is a den? It's a safe haven to hide yourself and other stuff personal to you. It's what people who can't let go of their childhood call the room where there's a big telly and a pool table and an electric guitar they never play.

But for all those who, in the playground of their minds, live perpetually in short trousers, a den is a hollow clearing behind some bushes or an old shed where they keep a biscuit tin full of secret codes and torches and ginger biscuits. And what's wrong with that? Well, maybe nothing if you're a kid, although having a secret place full of valuable things just makes other people want to barge their way in. Even *The Secret Seven*, Enid Blyton's U-certificate version of *The Famous Five*, had rivals who were always trying to nick the password and burst into the *Seven*'s shed.

Should you avoid having treasured possessions just because someone else might steal or damage them? Yes, of course. Take cars as an example. A BMW Z4 is asking to be nicked or scratched wherever you park it. Not many people know this but all brand-new Range Rovers come with a sticker underneath the back bumper which reads: 'What kind of jerk am I, spending fifty grand on a van? Feel free to trash it with impunity'. Owning a shitty Passat with no CD player and a layer of half-eaten children's food on the seats gives you guaranteed peace of mind. And don't hang a huge flat-scren telly on the wall of your living room; get an old cathode-ray tube job, deeper than it is wide. Stick it near the front window and it'll act as a positive deterrent to any gadget-hungry burglar.

If your kids must build a den, let them build it in their own bedrooms with some sofa cushions and a blanket draped over two chairs. They'll be safe there and they can read their collection of *Shoot!* magazines without fear of Malcolm Tully bursting in and snatching them off me, er, them.

• •

Make Your Own Seesaw

• •

I'll bet everyone reading this has tried at some point to make his or her own seesaw. On the face of it, it's simple; all you need is a wall and a long plank. But I'll also bet that everyone who tried to make their own seesaw realised it's one of the most lethal inventions ever to have taken shape in Man's brain, after the Brabantia slimline wastebin (have you tried removing a full bin-liner from one of those bastards?).

The first potential trap is the plank – it's never thick enough. As a floorboard it's fine; for fulcrum-based fun – useless. You balance the plank on the wall, the first person sits at one end, the other person puts his full weight on the other and the plank snaps, sending one of you plummeting to the ground arse-first.

You might think you're being smart by using a long ladder instead of a plank because it's reinforced by the rungs, but this only leads you into the second trap – the wall. The wall is always too high. Most seesaws balance on a pivot about two-foot-six high – who builds a wall that low? You are more likely to set up your seesaw on a wall surrounding a junk yard or playground or a garden wall. These tend to be built to keep people out so they are normally about five feet high. Supposing you manage to hinge the ladder on a five-foot wall and one of you gets up high enough to sit on the raised end of the seesaw. As soon as you do, the force with which the ladder swings your seesawing mate up is enough to catapult him twenty feet into the air, like a boulder from a medieval siege-engine. And because you will have forgotten to put something soft and spongy under each end of the plank or ladder, the impact of *your* backside on the ground will probably drive your coccyx into your kidneys.

Would you really feel a total fraud if you just went to the local playground and used a ready-made seesaw?

Start a Fire

If we are to believe King Louis in the *Jungle Book* the ability to light a fire is what sets us apart from the animals. But even if he's right I'm not going to beat myself up over the fact that, if I had to start my own fire from scratch without any matches, I'd end up just eating salads and vichyssoise. It may well have benefited mankind to know the secret of fire, if we're measuring our success by the existence of the grilled pork chop or the blast furnace, but the truth is fire is one of the good/bad things; one of those double-edged swords like the apple from the Tree of Knowledge which bring great power *and* great danger. According to the Ancient Greek myth, Prometheus stole the secret of fire from the gods and paid for it by having his liver pecked out by a vulture every day for three million years. So you can see that from the earliest times, the jury was out on whether humans could be trusted with fire – and that was before they invented napalm.

The religious awe in which fire is held can be seen in the way that people like Ray Mears or Bear Grylls, who know how to light fires from scratch, chastise anyone who is uninitiated – 'No! You don't do it like that! Never use paraffin! Where is your kindling? Feed a fire, don't smother it! Use newspaper to create an updraught, you dunderhead!'

Anyone old enough to remember the days before central heating will remember how many hours it took parents to start a fire – screwing up bits of newspaper laying twigs around it and putting the coal on top. And the hours it took to die down! Because you couldn't just turn a fire off and there was no way you would leave one burning while everyone was asleep. So you had to kick it out or rake it out or chuck sand on it or something. I reckon the amount of wasted energy from unwanted fires could have fuelled the Chinese economic boom.

Also, fire is bloody dangerous! Even when corralled into a tiny domestic fireplace it can reach out and damage you. How many people have fallen asleep next to a fire and woken up to find the skin on their shins has melted off? And just imagine how distraught I was when I left my Action Man's white cotton deep-sea diver's outfit on the clothes horse to dry, after an enjoyable afternoon's underwater exploration in the bath.

The heat from the fire scorched the material brown, except where the bars of the clothes horse got in the way, leaving the deep-sea diver's outfit with brown and white stripes. There was no way I could let Action Man go underwater looking like that so I had to invent a new character called Cat Man whose costume made him look like a tabby cat.

Yes, I know the Scouts, Guides and the Army only teach you how to light a fire in order to help you survive in the wilderness and cook beans and make coffee and keep the wolves away. But I'm going to gamble that when the shit really hits the fan and civilisation collapses, whether from Pig Flu, Dirty Bomb, Rising Sea Levels or Nuclear Winter, I'll manage to hook up with someone with a Zippo lighter. Or make my camp near a 24-hour garage and steal some firelighters and charcoal briquettes. There'll still be garages, won't there?

Tree Houses

I've written at great length about tree houses elsewhere (see *Can't Be Arsed*, still excellent value at £9.99), specifically about the strange hold the tree house has on the grown-up who wishes he was still a child. But everyone it seems wants a tree house: according to the *Dangerous Book For Boys*, 'alongside a canoe or a small boat, a tree house is the best thing you can have.'

Is it really?

Just what is so brilliant about a tree house? It can't be just that it's a den in a tree. And anyway, we know the problems with dens – people want to break in to them and take your stuff.

No, I think the allure of the tree house is that you're up high. Remember the kid from the *Singing Detective*? High up a tree, he's hiding from the nasty people on the ground and spying on people shagging – 'When I grow up I'm going to be a detective. I bloody be mind, I bloody damned buggerin' well be. And I shall curse. I'll find out things. I'll find out.' So in a tree house you can look down on other people and they can't see you – it's for nosey parkers and spies. Not a particularly healthy attitude to foster, is it?

And if you really want to take a leaf out of the boy in the *Singing Detective's* book, go ahead and climb a tree. Or if it's height and stability you're after, just get a good pair of stepladders and sit at the top. Hmm, maybe they're not so inconspicuous.

According to the Proper Childhood Police, a regular, plain-old tree house takes sixty man-hours to build and costs hundreds of pounds but is still 'healthier' than a computer game. Come off it – with a Nintendo Wii, you can be ready to play tennis or boxing in less than three minutes and you get a good physical work-out while you're at it. And I've never heard of anyone being injured with a nail-gun when setting up a Wii or getting splinters or falling twenty feet to their death while playing with it (OK, so someone tore their ankle ligaments playing Wii tennis in high-heels, but that guy was clearly an idiot).

Home Made Explosions

I've included this bit purely to put into perspective the philosophy of books that encourage children and childish adults to stick two fingers up to Health and Safety and take a few risks.

If you go back through the years you'll find many books that have urged children to get their hands dirty and find out about the real world by 'doing'. Many of these were published in the early part of the last century but they all really hark back to the *Boys' Own Book of 1829*, 'a complete encyclopedia of all the diversions'.

As well as giving you the rules for all sorts of really accessible sports like 'The Eton Wall Game', the *Boys' Own Book* showed you how to pull off spectacularly unwise stunts which both put to shame so-called 'dangerous' activities, like making a battery out of coins, and explain how a culture of health and safety has understandably grown up in this country.

If the argument is that the further back in time you go, the more fun children had, then the Victorian era must have been

Shangri-La for kids (the ones who weren't up chimneys or operating industrial looms, that is). Published on the eve of Victoria's reign, *The Boys' Own Book* has a fascinating chapter called 'Chemical Amusements', which aimed to 'direct the enquiring mind of youth to skim lightly and agreeably over the surface of chemistry'. In it the author liberally scatters the names of many lethal-sounding chemicals like saltpetre, tartar, oxymuriate of potash, nitrate of copper and semi-vitrified oxide of lead, which were clearly commonly available in those days. Was it really so dangerous? Or are we looking at it through the nanny-state funded Health and Safety goggles of the 21st century? Try this one:

An animal might be frozen to death in the midst of summer by being repeatedly sprinkled with ether.

OK, so a weasel gets frozen to death, it's only a bit of fun. How about this:

Put a small quantity of sulphuric acid into a glass or cup, and pour upon it about half its quantity of cold water: upon stirring it, the temperature will rise to many degrees above boiling water. In mixing sulphuric acid with water, great care should be taken not to do it too suddenly, as the vessel may break from the increased heat, and the acid be spilled on the hands, clothes, &c.

Well, it's only boiling water and sulphuric acid. There's nothing to worry about, clearly. Try this:

Pour a table-spoonful of oil of turpentine into a cup, and place it in the open air ; then put about half the quantity of nitric acid, mixed with a few drops

21

of sulphuric, into a phial, fastened to the end of a long stick ; pour it upon the oil, and it will immediately burst into flames, and continue to give out much light and heat.

Light and heat, you see. A valuable lesson, there.

The Boys' Own Book is a great read, hilarious *and* terrifying by turns, because we know that the children/people reading it for the first time in 1829 had no idea how big and bad the explosions and the chemical amusements were going to get in the next 180 years. And the other reason it's funny is that we know how incredulous the author of the book, William Clarke, would have been if there had been a health and safety executive in his day. I can hear the *Daily Mail* readers of 1829 now. 'It's an outrage! – the nanny state, political correctness gone mad! As a child, I swallowed bucketfuls of semi-vitrified oxide of lead and it didn't do me any harm.'

But is there anyone now who would deny that encouraging children to sprinkle ether on wildlife or boil up sulphuric acid in a crucible is a completely crazy thing to do? We have Health and Safety to keep our children healthy and safe. Next time you're thinking of playing conkers without safety goggles and gauntlets, remember that.

Fancy-dress Costumes

The most remarkable thing about home-made fancy dress is that, despite the psychological traumas that we (alright, just me) all suffered as children in various stupid costumes, there are still some adults out there who like nothing better than to spend good money making themselves look like a tit in public.

The earliest fancy-dress traumas are to do with not actually having the right costume. Weirdly most young kids seem really keen to go to their first ever party with a dress code, but can Mummy oblige with a decent outfit? This is where the ability to improvise creatively comes in handy because, as many fancy-dress books will tell you, the raw materials for any costume are close at hand and you can always get help on the internet.

Take these instructions for how to make a quick, simple home-made cowboy outfit:

You will need:

An old pair of jeans
Checked shirt
Handkerchief
Leather belt
Suede material
Needle
Thread
Scissors
Ten-gallon hat

Oh, a ten-gallon hat. I have that lying around, do I? There was me thinking that somehow you were going to show me how to make the hat. So the part of the costume that's the most difficult to make and the one thing without which it's not a cowboy costume – i.e. the hat – is achieved by buying the hat. Brilliant.

I've got a great idea for a home-made astronaut costume. All you need is scissors, sellotape, some buttons *and a fully functioning space suit from NASA.*

Whatever your Mum manages to knock up for you, within minutes of turning up to wherever the party is and checking out what everyone else is wearing, you'll wish you weren't dressed like that at all. Say you go as a pirate (about the easiest costume of all to make); you spot Karen Currie who is dressed as a princess, like all the other girls; Michael Winters is dressed like a cowboy and the rest of the boys have a football kit on – a total cop-out but you'll find out pretty soon that it was a smart move. Because for everything else that you need to do at the party, the costume gets in the way – chasing a balloon, pinning the tail on the donkey, eating cocktail sausages and cake, whatever. The bandana keeps coming off, you can't eat the food or chase a balloon with a hook and a cutlass, so you have to take them off and put them down, and you can't see properly with the eye patch, so for the rest of the afternoon you're not a pirate, just a boy in a striped T-shirt with the bottoms of your shorts savaged by pinking shears. Then it comes to the prize for the best costume and Richard Carter wins it for coming as George Best.

The catalogue of childhood disappointments associated with 'dressing up' is responsible for the involuntary shudder most normal people feel as grown-ups, when they hear the words: 'I'm having a party – it's fancy dress!' Unfortunately, this leads many people into the trap of trying to interpret the fancy-dress code in some sort of 'jokey' way. I understand why it happens but my advice is – just refuse to recognise the court; don't get involved with fancy dress at all; don't go to the party, de-bobble a jumper instead, anything.

Perhaps the worst ever example of a humorous take on the

fancy-dress code was perpetrated by some people at college, who were about to go to a big Knights and Damsels fancy-dress bash at the Students Union wearing all black, with black painted cardboard boxes over their heads. The cardboard boxes had strips cut out of them so the boxes looked like cages. When I asked them what they were going as they said they were the Dark Cages. I'll leave a respectful pause while you back away from that one.

Any attempt to make your own fancy dress, be it a child's cowboy outfit, or a student's piss-poor joke, involves cutting stuff up and poking needles and pins into things. All this highly skilled sharp-instrument work obviously brings physical injury that bit closer for the DIY costume-maker. This reminds me of one of my brothers who tried to make his own outfit for the school production of *Joseph and the Amazing Technicolor Dreamcoat*. He'd landed the part of Pharaoh – possibly the best part in the show for an extreme extrovert as it involved doing an extended Elvis-in-Vegas impression. He just happened to have a white safari suit (told you he was an extrovert) that would pass as one of The King's jump-suits, but felt that to complete the whole thing, he needed 'Elvis' written across the back in rhinestones. Not having any rhinestones he tried to make his own by chopping up a Christmas bauble with a Stanley knife. Unfortunately the knife slipped and he accidently dug the whole blade right into the end of his index finger. I remember the scream clearly as it sounded exactly like Tom from *Tom and Jerry*. As it turned out, Pharaoh's costume went down very well that year, although no-one could ever remember Elvis having such a huge bulbous white bandage on his index finger.

When bad things like that happen, the fancy-dress costume has the slightly spooky ability to cruelly mock the wearer. Just as when football fans with painted faces always look particularly ridiculous at Cup Finals when their team has lost and the tears have made all the colours run, so the fancily-dressed reveller can be reduced to a hopeless, pathetic, embarrassed pile of poop by the slightest downturn in fortunes. So, before you put on any fancy-dress costume just ask yourself – 'how forlorn will I look if I suddenly discover my wallet has been stolen or I see Jacqueline Tilley (dressed as a French maid) snogging Paul Walsh (dressed as a cat burglar)?'

Light Sabres

As a little cautionary postscript to 'Making your own fancy-dress', you ought to know about the disaster that awaits anyone trying to recreate costumes from contemporary folklore, like the *Star Wars* legend.

Now, you can buy pretty convincing light sabres in the shops. Some of them glow green, red *and* blue and make the definitive light sabre 'swoosh!' noise as you hurl and twirl it around. Admittedly some of these mock-ups cost upwards of £80, but even that would seem like a bargain to a couple of unfortunate *Star Wars* fans. As reported in a local newspaper not so long ago, in a town not so far away, two kids in Wales decided to make their own light sabres out of a couple of long neon strip-lighting tubes. Swinging large pieces of fragile glass around wasn't quite dangerous enough for these two loons, so they decided to fill the tubes with petrol and light them. The sabres began to glow in a most convincing way until the two lads crossed swords too enthusiastically, the tubes shattered and they were both showered with burning fuel. I'm not sure if they are out of hospital ... even now.

The Tin-can Telephone

Ah the old home-made favourite! And very easy, and safe, to make – none of this setting fire to glass tubes business. Get two empty tin cans. Most people will have baked bean tins but maybe for the authentically useless 1950s feel you should get a couple of tins of Batchelor's marrowfat peas, Libby's peaches

or Tyne Brand minced meat pie-filling ('no lumps of fat or gristle *guaranteed*').

So, cut the lids off the tins. Ideally these will have been removed by one of those old-fashioned tin-openers with the bendy spike, which you are meant to jam in and twist around until you've hacked out a jagged circle of tin, with plenty of sharp edges to give you a nasty cut.

Take each empty tin and pierce a hole in the centre at the bottom. You'll probably try to do this with a hammer and a nail and the nail will bend sideways or bounce off and hit you in the face or the hammer will slip and smack you on the thumb.

Once you've got the tin cans with the holes in the bottom, take a long piece of string – make sure it is long – and tie a big knot in one end, any kind of knot (see page 106). Poke the string down inside one of the tins, being careful as you do so not to catch your knuckles on the jagged edges where the tin was opened. Push the unknotted end of the string through the hole and pull it through on the other side. You should now have a long piece of string – make sure you have made it a long piece – coming out of the bottom of one tin which, if you pull it tight, will be held inside the tin by the knot. If it doesn't hold tight, you'll have to do it all again, getting more cuts in the process.

When you finally get the knot tied properly on the first can, you need to thread the free end of the string – it *is* a long piece of string isn't it? – through the hole in the bottom of the other can, but from the outside. Got it? Push it through far enough to come out inside the second can, reach inside – getting more cuts in the process – and tie another knot in the free end of the string[1].

Both tin cans should be connected. What you now need to do is get a friend to hold one tin can, while you hold the other and you both walk apart from each other until the string between the tin cans is tight. Not too tight or the string will get pulled out of ... oh, it has. OK, start the whole thing again ...

TWO HOURS LATER...

So you and your friend now have a tin can each, with a taut length of string – quite a good length, I hope – between you. You should now speak into your tin, trying to avoid cutting your face on the jagged edges, while your friend puts his ear to *his* tin,

[1]After you have cut yourself often enough by this method you will eventually realise you could have avoided all the bloodshed by threading both cans from the outside before trying either of the knots.

trying to avoid cutting *his* ear on the jagged edges, and listens.

The theory is that the sound waves of the voice travel down the vibrations of the taut string and are amplified by the tin at the other end, so you can speak and listen to each other from a distance.

But what actually happens is, because you haven't made the string long enough *LIKE I TOLD YOU*, you can hear each other quite clearly anyway as you're only ten feet apart. You might as well just stand at opposite ends of the garden and shout at each other. All that bloody work for nothing! All that tin-opening and knot-tying and cutting yourself on the sharp tin edges and for what? And because the tins were probably made in the 1950s they are probably very rusty and contaminated with tetanus and you're going to get lockjaw and die.

Whittling Wood

When I came home from school in the 1970s the first thing I did was put the television on. Television is brilliant for kids – it is now and it always was. CBeebies and CBBC showcase the work of geniuses and when I was a child ITV did too. There was one particularly brilliant programme called *How?* It was a cross between *Tomorrow's World*, *Record Breakers* and *Animal Magic* and was basically a treasure trove of general knowledge for kids. Can you imagine ITV broadcasting anything like that now? One of the presenters on *How?* was Jack Hargreaves, an amiable old codger with a fantastic white beard, who was in fact a brilliant, smart and highly creative media mogul from North London, who had immersed himself in folklore and 'the old ways'. However brilliant he was, though, Jack's bits were always by far the most boring part of the show. While one of the other presenters was showing you how rockets worked, a typical Jack Hargreaves item would be 'How does moss grow?' or 'How do you preserve soft fruits?'

Jack's real passion appeared to be wood. So much so that almost every episode of his solo series *Out of Town* opened on Jack in a shed with 'some marvellous examples of the whittler's craft'. If I turned on the TV after school to find *Out of Town* with Jack Hargreaves was on, it was enough to make me do my homework. I'd still rather watch it than Paul O'Grady or Alan Titchmarsh, mind.

Anyway, for this reason, wood-whittling has always struck me as the most tedious way to pass the time. Like angling, there is supposed to be some virtue in the patience you need to keep shaving away at the lump of pine in your hand and the trance-like, contemplative state that whittling induces in the whittler is supposed to be equivalent to that of the devotees of Khali. Well, maybe, but if you've ever tried sharpening a pencil with the edge of a spoon rather than a proper sharpener you'll get some idea of the difficulty and pointlessness of it.

Granted there are some very talented people out there who can whittle entire villages of trolls and gnomes out of humble lumps of limewood, but most people would struggle to generate a single shaving without gashing themselves.

Here's how wood-whittling experts would advise you to approach the task – I've spoken to a few and they're all crackers.

Look at the wood and decide what you want to whittle – think about what the wood wants. A piece of wood will speak to you – telling you that the new shape already exists, deep within the wood. It's the whittler's job to let it out.

All I can hear the wood saying to me is – go and watch the telly or play FIFA '09 on the PlayStation, it'll be much more fun than this. Because the truth is, wood is nice to look at but deeply boring to play with. (see Wooden Toys p75)

Paper Aeroplanes

There are dozens and dozens of different designs for paper aeroplanes. All of them crap. They all operate on the basic principle of trying to catch the air currents under as large a wing surface area as possible.

To launch the paper aeroplane, you need to project it at an angle no greater than 27 degrees. If you follow the instructions exactly you are guaranteed the same result every time...

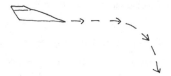

There are planes which are assembled in two parts and there are planes which consist of just a couple of folds in the paper, but the laws of aerodynamics require that the basic structure finishes in a point like this:

which after a couple of throws is modified into a shape like this:

Why Can't Home-made Fun Involve Electricity?

What is it about home-made fun that's supposed to be so much better than pre-packaged amusement? It's all to do with the Doctrine of the Imagination, which will come up again in the next chapter.

In short the argument goes: if you make something yourself you must engage your brain and your imagination at the same time, no doubt because you'll have to pretend that the piece of junk you've nailed together was in some way worth the effort. It seems though, that for all those who lament the disappearance of the soap-box cart, the tree house and the home-made bow and arrow, modern uses of the imagination simply will not do.

So making your own movie with a mini DV camera and a computer is unacceptable then? What about writing your own computer programs and producing your own video game? What about making a stop-frame animation with some plasticine and a digital camera? What about writing and recording your own song on a digital sound-suite like Garageband?

Are the people who do that – mainly boys, it has to be said – are those boys merely socially inadequate, pasty-faced geeks because their imagination keeps them indoors and away from the dangers of whittling knives and go-cart accidents?

It's said that anxious parents are restricting the freedom of kids to experiment and run risks, but there's a new anxiety of a different kind, displayed by parents who are so worried that their kids will not amuse themselves in the *correct* way that their eyes and arms and brains will atrophy. And so we end up with a list of 'acceptable' ways for people to have fun, which can be neatly described as Wholesome Entertainment...

Non Essential Kit for Boys:

A Pen-knife

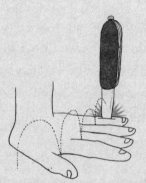

Every normal fun-loving boy is supposed to have an essential kit of stuff to carry with them at all times to enable them to indulge in various 'dangerous' activities. What they don't realise is that the Essential Kit is like a cocktail of ingredients capable of resulting in major catastrophe, disaster and loss of life, or a spell in the slammer. A bit like Robert Wagner and Stefanie Powers in *Hart To Hart* – 'When they met it was moider'.

Every boy should have a pen-knife, apparently. Of course they should! Yes, don't let the mandatory five-year jail sentence deter you – keep a pen-knife with you at all times, because you never know when you may have to whittle something in an emergency or carve Boy Scout code into a tree. That's if there's room on the tree between the usual stuff like 'Shaneez is a Slag' and 'Stoggsy is gay'; not much reliance on code there.

I imagine it might be a bit of 'dangerous' fun dodging round the metal detectors on your way into school or avoiding the stop and search on your way home. Perhaps you should keep a stab vest in your essential kit too, in case someone else with a knife thinks they need 'protecting' from you.

Of course, not all stab wounds are fatal; some nicks with a dirty blade will just give you septicaemia. A good way to pick up one of these 'nicks' is to play that schoolboy favourite, the Five Finger Fillet. You know the one – Bishop the android from the film *Aliens* performs it at high speed. Put your palm on the table and spread out your fingers, then stab the table in between each gap between the fingers, going faster and faster until you draw blood or, in Bishop's case, milk.

Actually a pen-knife is probably the worst tool for this job, as the faster you go, the more likely the blade will fold back in on itself trapping the fingers of your stabbing hand. But imagine the fun you'll have until then.

Chapter Two
Wholesome Entertainment

The problem with today's society, goes a familiar argument, is that children just don't know how to be bored these days. There is too much stimulation from TV and computer games and not enough 'down time'. Children, say the experts, need to be bored so their imagination will kick in, leading them into areas of play and experimentation which will encourage their mental development far more effectively than an hour or two of Mario Kart on the Wii.

It's true; being bored encourages you to experiment and try new stuff. When I was a kid that meant trying stuff like 'How many stairs can I jump down without breaking a leg?' or 'I wonder how many dried peas I can stick in my earhole?' or 'How long can I hang by a noose from the banisters before I pass out?' and 'Would anything really happen if I drank this entire bottle of turps?'

Any teacher will tell you that the most dangerous time of day is lunch break when it's raining. A classroom full of bored children on a rainy day has the same potential for catastrophe as sticking an electric toothbrush into a wasps' nest. To stop this happening these days, teachers put videos on. Yes, videos! How fantastic. Because in the 60s, when I went to primary school, all we had to entertain ourselves with were comics and fighting. Yes, our imaginations were called upon to do a bit of overtime, and like all the brilliant minds in human history, that time was put to use devising methods of torture.

One particularly medieval diversion was the 'Tunnel of Death': about twenty kids lean against a wall with arms outstretched forming a tunnel under their arms, then other kids take it in turns to run through the tunnel while the tunnel-formers kick the shit out of them. If you go down, everyone stamps on you until you manage to crawl out. There was an older variation of this where two rows of boys faced one another seated on cloakroom benches, and they would kick their legs out viciously as the victim walked between the two rows. Again the object was not to fall down or you would be swallowed up in the boiling sea of thrashing legs and shoes, studded with Segs or Blakeys[1] – depending on where you were brought up.

I don't know if this sort of stuff still happens – if not, that will be because teachers *do* play videos on wet days, or because every kid has a Nintendo DS or a G3 mobile in their pocket to keep them stimulated, or because they save up their aggression for the after-school knife fights. But my childhood was clouded by horrific tales of bizarre childhood injuries normally sustained during an attempt to alleviate boredom.

[1] Metal tips you hammered into the heel of your shoe to make it last longer and create sparks as you shuffled along. Not recommended for trainers.

One legend had it that a twelve-year-old boy attempted to impress his friends by leaping over the coat-peg partitions between the benches in the school cloakroom, only to impale himself on a peg – right through the scrotum. There were also tales of one kid in an athletics session getting hit by a javelin in the eye; another being hit in the throat by a discus, and I definitely heard the nose of Michael Harrison break on the side of my head during a game of rugby (more on this, page 62).

But perhaps my favourite injury tale of all concerns me. My brother and I (brothers often witness each other's accidents, don't they?) were mucking around in the garden trying to throw a cricket ball at each other's head. We were bored, you see, and our imaginations had kicked in. After I'd ducked one of my brother's particularly hard throws I went to the flowerbed to retrieve the ball for my shot. As I bent down – quite quickly as I wanted to get my retaliation in fast – the dried-up stem of a hydrangea plant went straight up my left nostril. Luckily for me, although there was sufficient force to draw quite a lot of blood, the hydrangea stem wasn't quite long enough to penetrate my brain. What a way to go. Imagine having that on your death certificate. Killed by a flower.

So, let's not overestimate the value of a vivid imagination. It's strange to see how electronic media such as computers, televisions and games consoles are demonised today by older people, especially as they would all have loved to have had them when they were kids. But since the generation of people who are now publishing nostalgia books can still remember the days of clockwork, wood, springs, elastic bands and tiddlywinks, 'traditional' games are the only means of entertainment they believe to be suitable for children. But let's take a closer look at just how useless some of these were ...

Pencil and Paper Games

The advantage of pencil and paper games – and, let's be fair, pencil and paper in general – is that there's always a good excuse for having them with you, especially at school. So, convincing Sir that you were doing algebra was pretty easy, whereas in fact you were playing dab cricket or battleships. The rubbish thing about pencil and paper games however is that – noughts and crosses aside – they take so bloody long to play. Here are some of the most effective ways to waste your time :

Battleships
Come on, who has ever played a game of Battleships until the very last submarine's been sunk? The actual Battle of Jutland took less time to complete. If you were playing against Dennis McGlynn – who only sat next to you in French – you would probably have gained an 'O' level before you'd managed to hit his destroyer. In fact so much time is spent waiting for people to take their shot in Battleships that you might as well not play anything but just stare into space.

Othello
This is the game – a bit like draughts – in which your black pieces are meant to surround your opponent's white ones and 'flip' them so they change colour.

The Dangerous Book For Boys actually recommends playing

Othello on paper, but there is so much rubbing out involved every time a piece changes colour that the paper will have disintegrated before either player has bagged a corner. I feel I have to point out, as well as being available in plastic board-game form, there's a really good version of Othello on the internet that you can play on a mobile phone. You don't even need to sit next to Dennis McGlynn, you could play him if he was in China. Which is, in fact, where he is now.

Dots

You have to start by painstakingly pencilling a grid of 64 dots. You may think that this sounds like a rather boring prelude to a fun game and you'd be half right. It *is* a boring prelude but there is no fun to follow. After you have wasted half a day setting up, both players spend the first three hours of actually playing the game trying to avoid mistakes. Then someone does and oh, it's game over and you realise you'd have had more fun getting the hairs out of a plughole.

Sprouts

More dot-joining, but at least it doesn't waste as much time as Dots. In fact you can draw as many dots as you like, then draw a line from one dot to another, putting another dot in the middle of that line but remembering that no dot can have more than three lines coming off it. Are you still with me? Actually there's an interesting mathematical formula to calculate the number of possible moves which is $((\text{dots}-1) \times 3) + 2$ ... hello ...? hello ...? where've you gone? Come back!

Wholesome Entertainment

Hangman

OK, I'll admit, Hangman is a pretty good way to pass the time. But I still have to rule it out on 'dangerous' grounds because tempers are known to have been raised and blows exchanged by the insistence of some players that the gallows and body of the hangee have about twenty-three extra bits on them.

This is what most normal people would accept as the completed hangman; simple and no-nonsense:

And this is the hangman of an extrememly irritating pedant called Dominic Beaton from 4S at St Wilfrid's R.C. High School, Featherstone (1977):

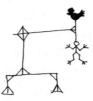

Dab Cricket

Write down some cricket scores (4, 6, 3, single) and some ways of getting out (caught, bowled, run-out after third umpire video replay) on a sheet of paper and turn the paper over. For every bowler's 'delivery', stick your pen in the back of the paper and see what the outcome is. In the time it takes to watch a normal test match you might have completed the first innings. I hate to keep suggesting this but a few clicks of the mouse will take you to Stick Man Cricket on the internet, which is loads better.

Board Games

Cluedo

The packaging is everything with *Cluedo*. The floor plan, the characters, the little representations of the weapons and their creepy photographs – that half-tone image surrounded by a misty oval of darkness on a black background, like a Hitchcock close-up from *Blackmail*. It's lucky the packaging is so good because as entertainment Cluedo is utter crap. Most people have no grasp of the basic process of elimination you need to win the game – they cross a few rooms off, hop between the conservatory and the kitchen a few times, copy what everyone else is doing ('He keeps accusing The Reverend Green – it must be him!'), rashly make an accusation and find when they open the secret envelope – oh dear! – they have got the weapon and the room right but the person's wrong – it wasn't The Reverend Green after all! Of course, if your accusation fails you're out, but the game still goes on for ages, like the bit of *Deal or No Deal* after someone's won the money. But when it's over and you feel like there should be another game to give you a second chance, no-one's interested any more because it's all been a bit tiresome.

I was so blinded to the boredom by the wonderful packaging that even though none of my brothers could be arsed, I would actually try to play Cluedo on my own, pretending to be all the other players. I soon realised that once I had made my accusation and looked in the envelope I had to pretend to forget it. How sad is that? I also foolishly tried to see how sharp the little dagger really was by poking it into the palm of my hand – it was sharp enough. Not everyone is that stupid, but even now the game does create a morbid curiosity among children who, before they came across Cluedo, had never realised there were so many ways to kill people –'Dad, why is a candlestick a weapon? How does lead piping kill you?' Most kids wouldn't think to go beyond the obvious Glock semi-automatic pistol or butterfly knife. Thanks to Cluedo they may well be tempted to see if a candlestick will set off the school metal-detector.

The other unnerving development associated with games such as Cluedo is the rise of the Collector Nerd. Like Monopoly, Cluedo has appeared in many different forms throughout the world and there are some people out there who have collected every single edition of Cluedo ever and have websites with page upon page of different depictions of Miss Scarlett, some of them pretty raunchy. I'll be honest, I was interested enough to look at this stuff for a couple of minutes – but then I stumbled on to another part of the site, where the guys explain how they have invented their very own versions of Cluedo with additional room, weapon and 'motive' cards such as:

Who: The Reverend Green
Where: The bedroom
Weapon: Silk scarf
Motive: Auto-erotic Asphyxia

Some of them have even made their own extra floors of the

house out of cardboard. I wouldn't be surprised if one or two of them have turned their own real-life house over to the game and they're just waiting to lure a Cluedo-curious internet browser round to their place for a spot of real murder.

Scrabble

The last resort of someone trying to salvage a dull evening. We will know for sure that television in this country is well and truly up the creek, when sales of Scrabble start going up. To be fair, we all like to show off our vocabulary, don't we? We all enjoy showing how much we know in a competitive context, and Scrabble is a good way of doing that. It also promotes resourcefulness when you are struggling with four Es, two As and a Q. But winning at Scrabble because you know the list of two-letter words for printing terms or three-toed sloths is worthy only of scorn and derision. The people who use them have no idea what they mean – they know they don't need to know and they're proud of it. This is from a Scrabble fans' website, called The Phrontistery – from the ancient Greek *phrontistes* meaning 'twat'.

Knowing which words are acceptable – even if you have no idea of their definitions – is a perfectly legitimate strategy and an excellent way to improve your play.

I think you'll agree that the use of the word 'acceptable' here is not remotely legitimate.

This kind of attitude in a game of Scrabble can lead to all sorts of problems like raised blood-pressure, shouting, swearing etc. and the painful realisation that the person you thought you knew is really a tragic anorak; the sort of person who would know that the word anorak scores 206 on a triple-word score. (I looked it up, OK?)

Chess

What do you want from your life? Be really honest with yourself – it's to not be the spaz of the group, isn't it? You want to be quite good at stuff; you don't have to be the best as long as you are not obviously the worst. That's all anyone wants, for themselves and their kids – to be normal and average. Who really wants to be the absolute best at everything? If you ever meet anyone like that, steer well clear.

Unfortunately, you can't be just average at chess. As a grown up, the best you can hope for is to spar playfully at chess with your child until they reach that point where suddenly the switch goes on, they get it and bang! You are chess toast. Equally, it can dawn on them that they don't get it, so they'll probably give up. No point trying to compete with the chess Sith at school if they're going to be massacred in five minutes. You might keep a chess set at home for really dull days when even Scrabble can't be contemplated, but you'll probably bore each other to death with your futile attempts to hang on to your queen for as long as possible. This is a common mistake, according to online chess boffins – chess is about sacrifice.

The other thing chess boffins know about is 'openings' – set plays to start off the game and put you ahead of your opponent. This is intensely annoying. You move one pawn and they say: 'Ah, the Ruy Lopez opening!' whereas you have no idea what you're doing; you've got to bloody well move something. They will announce that they will counter with what they call the 'Nimzo-Larsen Attack' to which you should say, 'I don't like Heavy Metal bands'. Like the Scrabble players who know all the two-letter words, they are nothing more than cheats. No normal person starts a game of chess knowing what their tenth move will be.

People who are good at chess in films tend to like Bach and organise bank heists with meticulous precision. They are also good at maths (see p152 for the danger of maths) and always manage to get off with Faye Dunaway in *The Thomas Crown Affair*. This is in stark contrast to what happens to most people who are good at maths and spend a lot of time playing chess. At my school, these kids used to get their ears flicked and failed to get off with anyone, even each other. Unfortunately the image of *Thomas Crown Affair*-type chess genius still lures many a poor fool into taking up the game and, in the end, making a wally[1] of himself.

If you must play chess, play it on a computer and set it to 'idiot'. It will do wonders for your self-esteem, unless, of course, it beats you, but at least no one will know.

Monopoly

Never ever has a game of Monopoly been played to the end without at least one serious row, possibly with blood being drawn. Because although it teaches you quite a few lessons about budgeting, spending within your means, forward planning etc. the main lesson is Capitalism Is Bad. And Monopoly teaches you this lesson by constantly showing how readily your opponents will shit on you. People spend money on stupid investments and the lucky ones get to take the idiots to the cleaners. These idiots are then forced to remortgage their own properties or borrow from the other players, who can

[1] I like that word – time to bring it back.

charge whatever interest they like. Some of the others are stealing from the Bank while others aren't looking and only the unlucky ones go to jail. It's a pretty accurate representation of the free-market system but even though Monopoly has mutated into hundreds of different versions, the format of the game can't quite accommodate modern concepts of Quantitative Easing or Securitised Debt Obligation. There is no square you can land on, or Chance card you can pick up that says – 'A stupid investment bank buys your package of sub-prime mortgages for a squillion pounds. Collect a large bottle of champagne, several mansions and a brand-new Bentley. Go to the top of the nearest building and piss on all the other suckers below who will pick up the tab for you in three years' time.'

Perhaps the most realistic version of Monopoly was the illegal spin-off Ghettopoly, in which the players took the part of drug dealers and made their fortune from running down their neighbourhoods instead of building them up. This probably hit the morality nail squarely on the head.

So I would avoid Monopoly. It's dangerous partly because of the arguments it causes, but mainly because it tells you so starkly what a screwed-up world we all live in that you may actually want to top yourself.

Risk

As a middle-aged man I am opposed to risk in principle, generally preferring the quiet life. Had this been the case when I was eighteen then I would have embraced the board game of Risk as it is one of the dullest things you can do with cardboard and dice. 'I am going to risk invading Irkutsk by throwing a six' Whoa! Easy, tiger!

I remember in my first year at university wondering what sort of life I had let myself in for when, on a Saturday night in February, the other students I was hanging around with suggested we spend the evening playing Risk. It was proposed quite tentatively, almost shame-facedly by one of the group, as if he'd really had to pluck up the courage to do it, and was suggesting something really embarrassing like we all tried each other's underpants on. It is a measure of how limited my options for socialising were then, that I was still in the room when the Risk box was opened. The rest of the evening is lost in a fug of tedium. All I can remember is someone attacking Kamchatka – which sounds much more exciting than it was.

I imagined the world passing me by outside the windows of the student room we were in and thought: this isn't what it was like in *Brideshead Revisited*. I'm meant to have Sebastian Flyte puking on my carpet, while Boy Mulcaster is debagged and dipped in the fountain. But shortly afterwards I encountered some late twentieth-century incarnations of Sebastian and Boy Mulcaster at close quarters, many of whom actually were regularly swapping each other's underpants. I think I actually made the right decision to stay with the Risk syndicate. Nevertheless while everyone pretended, after the game had finished, that it had been more fun than we'd expected, deep down we all felt ashamed. We never spoke again about the Saturday night we stayed in and played Risk and I've never lifted the lid on it since.

Snakes and Ladders

This is always on the reverse side of Ludo. One board, two games – that tells you all you need to know. Both games are too useless to survive on their own.

People have tried to jazz Ludo up with the 'Popomatic' dice shaker and call it 'Frustration' but they're not fooling anyone. It's still shit. How many people have got the first counter round and thought: 'I really can't be arsed to get the other three out'? And is it the exact number on the dice to get home or can you throw over? This is the big question for all board games and I don't think it's ever been properly sorted out. What do they *do* at the G8 summit?

There's a structural flaw in Snakes and Ladders, namely the way the numbers run in a boustrophedon. Yes, I thought you'd be annoyed about that too, and the man from The Phrontistery has probably just wet himself. A Boustrophedon is an ox-plough track which sort of doubles back on itself – so on the Snakes and Ladders board, 1 – 10 goes from left to right, 11 – 20 goes from right to left. Did you notice that? Probably not – and all this time you've been jumping from 11 – 21 without thinking about it. Aren't you ashamed?

Snakes and Ladders holds a special place in the heart of those who beat the drum for a 'Proper Childhood' because of its origins. It's basically a morality tale for children and the earliest board illustrations showed kids doing selfish things at the top of snakes like stealing apples from a tree. The bottom of the snake usually depicted the punishment for the child – a nasty fall and a bump on the head, or better still, eternal damnation and weeping and gnashing of teeth. Good deeds like watering the garden for Mummy sent you to the top of the ladder with a big cuddle at the end. And there are actually more snakes than ladders proving, as Virgil said, 'how easy is the descent to hell!'. That's Virgil the poet, not the pilot of Thunderbird 2.

If the very thought of this makes your wooly, middle-class liberal blood boil, then take comfort from the fact that this moral instruction will undoubtedly fail. If all children are like mine, the goody-goodies in the illustrations at the tops of ladders will have no appeal for them whatsoever. The idea of nicking apples, then sliding down a long snake to crack your head open at the bottom would have my kids desperate to land on a serpent's head. Equally they are pretty good at spotting smugness in another child's face, so the goody-goodies at the top of the ladders will have as much appeal for them as Horrid Henry's brother Perfect Peter.

Dangerous Book For Boys Games

The Dangerous Book For Boys has been so successful it has now become what really annoying people call a 'brand'. You can stick the 'Dangerous Book For Boys' logo on to almost anything and it will sell. I don't blame the authors for this – they wrote their book for themselves and never expected it to succeed. But now the 'Brand' has got out of hand – everything from poetry to chunks of British history has received the 'Dangerous' benediction and nowhere is it more cynically used than in the games and toys market. What kind of game do you think is worthy of the 'Dangerous' label?

Tiddlywinks.

Yes, tiddlywinks. Leaving aside the fact that tiddlywinks are made of plastic and therefore surely *verboten* in the dewy-eyed land of 'Proper Childhood', by what measure is a game of tiddlywinks 'dangerous'? There's no other reason than the fact that tiddlywinks are old-fashioned fun, like marbles and trainspotting – the sort of things Winker Watson and Jennings and the boys from *Just William* would do in between 'wizard wheezes'. There is also a specially designed *Dangerous Book For Boys* board game that involves answering questions about knots and winning bits of a raft to escape from a pirate island. It's a neat symbol for what the DBFB marketing machine is trying to achieve – nostalgia masquerading as education and self-improvement. So now we have 'Dangerous' magic tricks, science experiments, card tricks, indeed anything so long as it doesn't require electricity. Unless, of course, you generate it yourself by building your own water mill, or from the batteries you have made with blotting paper and vinegar (see p9).

Trivial Pursuit

Not sure whether this counts as a proper board game for the Nostalgia Police as it emerged after the Second World War, but as it's now over thirty years old it's probably acceptable to them. You can actually find people who will lament the passing of our obsession with Trivia as if it were the last Routemaster Bus on its way to the scrapheap. There was a time, they say, when Trivia meant something in a serious, grown-up world; when Trivia was a little parcel of irrelevant and useless knowledge that could be treasured for its very uselessness. But now, they say, we are surrounded by useless irrelevant crap every day as the world has gone mad for dumbed-down news, celebrity culture and reality TV. They may have a point but if we start getting misty-eyed over an 80s board game we're in big bloody trouble.

On balance, I'm giving the thumbs down to Trivial Pursuit, simply for creating one of the most pointless disputes ever – what to call the thing you win if you get a question right. Piece, segment, orange, cake, cheese, pie, slice, wedge or pizza? I have followed the thread about this subject on a Questions-Answered website and there were about two hundred posts, with the level of abuse rising with each one.

There's no argument – it's a pie.

Dingbats

Many people will confuse this with the silly typeface (or am I thinking of Wingdings?) but, no, Dingbats is another of those 80s board games that doesn't need a board (see below) and is a cross between Roy Walker's appalling TV quiz *Catchphrase* and cryptic crosswords. I'm not sure there's been a worse combination since Corden and Horne hosted the Brits. Let's deal with *Catchphrase* first. Roy Walker, a mild and inoffensive comedian (does that make him offensively mild?) tested the brains of his contestants with word and picture clues to certain well-known phrases. E.g. he would show a picture of a hand with a bird in it next to a bush with two birds in it. Then Roy would utter his own personal catchphrase – 'say what you see', to which the correct answer is always 'I see crap television', but the contestant would say something staggering like 'Bush-hand bird!'

Now, hold that thought in your head if you can, and mix it with the smugness and arrogance of cryptic crosswords. I'll make no secret of the fact that I have never been able to solve cryptic crossword clues. Actually, I don't believe anyone anywhere really knows how to do them. The clues are made up and so are the answers. E.g.

Laden forester backs into Whitstable – I doubt it!' (7 letters)

Answer: Fish.

Cryptic crossword compilers and completers are lauded for their ingenuity and planet-sized brains, but really they're just messing about with a set of conventions and traditional 'indicators' which, once you've learned them, make solving cryptic crosswords easy – except that, as I've said, they're all made up. Just put anything you like.

In the post-Trivial Pursuit boom, when everyone was supposed to be playing happy families around a board game, opportunistic games manufacturers were looking for anything they could nail a board and dice on to and charge people £30 for at Christmas. Most of these were old parlour games, which you'll find are even more yearned-after than board games by the Nostalgia Police.

Balderdash
Balderdash is a board-game version of *Call My Bluff*, which is in turn a TV panel-show version of an old parlour game called Dictionary, which involves leafing through a dictionary for two hours trying to find an obscure word that no one knows the definition of until you realise that *Call My Bluff* uses the full-on bells-and-whistles Complete Oxford English Dictionary while

you only have the Collins Pocket Dictionary For Idiots with words like 'cat' and 'shoe' being about the most obscure you can find. I wonder how many houses in Britain have no dictionary at all.

Pictionary

This is a simple game where you communicate ideas by trying to draw them, for which the board and the dice is completely irrelevant. The dead giveaway is the category choice.

O = object
P = person/place/animal or any noun (is this really different from 'object?')
A = action
D = difficult (what's that? Anything from the previous three?)
AP = All Play (basically anything at all)

Guessture

A board game based on Charades. Why not just play Charades? Because it's rubbish.

Articulate

It's a board game of an old parlour game called, rather unimaginatively, What Am I Describing? You may know it as The Name Game, where you have to communicate a series of names to your team without using rhymes or pointing. This can lead to quite a lot of frustration and anger, plus rather a lot of pointing and the exchange of quite a few names.

Procrastinate

I've made this one up, especially for Christmas. Players take it in turns to put off playing any stupid board games until *Wallace and Gromit* comes on the telly.

• •

Parlour Games

• •

Just in case you are tempted to play any 'classic' parlour games of the 1930s and re-enact the hours of fun that kept people entertained back then, in between the abdications of monarchs on the radio and someone playing the piano badly, here is a list of the really rubbish ones that actually existed. Go crazy …

Change Seats!

Everyone sits on chairs in a circle and the person who is 'it' tries to steal one of the seats by saying something that will get at least two people out of their chairs and running around – 'He's sleeping with your wife' would probably do it.

Lookabout

Everyone leaves the room and the person who is 'it' hides an object somewhere then everyone comes back in and desperately tries to find it – it should be an object that is highly prized and everyone would want, like the key to the drinks cabinet or the TV remote.

There's a variation on this called **Hot Boiled Beans**, where one person hands over an object, then leaves the room while it is hidden. When this person comes back in he starts looking for the object while everyone shouts, 'Hot Boiled Beans and Bacon for supper, hurry up before it gets cold.' To which the appropriate response is, 'D'you know what? I'll leave it.'

Yet another variation is called **Pan Tapping.**

When the outside player returns he is guided towards the task he must perform by one of the players who has been given a pan and a spoon. This player taps faster and louder as the outsider gets closer to the object he needs to use for the task and taps slower and softer as the outsider moves away from it. This continues until the outsider finds the object or everyone else seizes the pan tapper and stoves his head in.

I'm Thinking of Something

A very simple party game like Animal, Vegetable or Mineral where one person says, 'I'm Thinking of Something – Guess What It Is'. It's probably 'Please, let me go home'.

The Laughing Game

All players sit in a circle. One player starts the game by saying 'Ha'. Then, going around the circle, the second player says 'Ha Ha', third player says 'Ha Ha Ha', and so on. All players must not laugh or smile, but must proceed with straight faces. Or, more likely, stony faces.

Poor Pussy

One player is chosen to be 'pussy' and all the other players sit in a circle. Pussy walks around the inside of the circle on hands and knees and then adopts a begging position at the feet of one chosen person in the circle. Pussy tries to look as pitiful as possible and must cry out a mournful 'meow' sound. This challenging game hadn't been played since Victorian times until it was reintroduced at Guantanamo Bay as the prelude to 'waterboarding'.

The Minister's Cat

You'll remember that Scrooge, in the Albert Finney version of *A Christmas Carol*, sees his nephew's friends playing a Christmas party game that looks like such fun that he's desperate to join in. The game is The Minister's Cat. I won't bother explaining the rules, suffice to say after about an hour everyone will be chanting this: 'The Minister's Cat is a loquacious cat, the minister's cat is a lugubrious cat, the minister's cat is a lackadaisical cat ....' If I'd have been Scrooge I would have been begging the scary Ghost of Christmas Future to take me back to Tiny Tim's grave.

This tells you all you need to know about how boring life was in those days, because if The Minister's Cat and the like were a way of alleviating boredom, the outbreak of War must have come as a light relief. In fact, it's not stretching the point too far to suggest that having to play the likes of Hot Boiled Beans and Bacon or dab cricket with a pencil and paper actually *encouraged* people to kick off a global conflagration.

Non Essential Kit for Boys:

A Box of Matches

Now what else would a boy do with a box of matches other than start a fire? Light all the candles for the priest in their local church? Set the stove going for the friendly neighbourhood inventor to boil up tar for his moon rocket?

Give any boy a box of matches and some kind of arson is the first idea that pops into his mind. When I was a kid I loved lighting fires; one of the most interesting words I knew was pyromaniac. I might have been about nine years old when I sneaked a hand into the kitchen drawer and sneaked off with a box of Captain Webb's finest – bearing the eminently sensible legend 'keep away from children' – and made a real good go of setting light to my dad's garage.

I was a persistent little fellow and although it took me half a box to realise you had to shelter the newly-lit match from the breeze with your other hand, and another quarter of a box to find anything combustible, I soon had a nice blaze going. I was bored on this particular day, you see, and my imagination had kicked in, like it's supposed to. In my imagination I saw the huge ball of twine in the corner next to the can of 3-in-1 oil become a blazing beacon, visible for miles around and bright enough to warn of a Napoleonic invasion. In fact it could quite easily have ended up doing that: my dad, as it happened, was illegally hoarding two giant jerry-cans full of petrol in his garage in defiance of the 70s oil shortage. Fortunately I began to 'brick it' well before the flames reached the fuel-dump and scurried back ashen-faced to the kitchen to tell my mother, 'I've done something wrong.'

A box of matches was like a miniature selection of Standard fireworks for me, and my older brothers had no shortage of pyrotechnical stunts for me to copy. E.g. wrap the head of the match in tin foil – fag paper from a box of Embassy No.6 will do – and balance it on the end of the matchbox; light another match, heat up the foil and bang! The match will shoot out at high velocity and probably catch your dog in the eye.

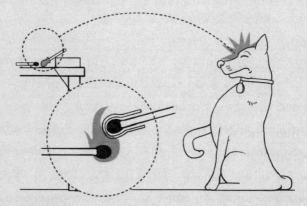

There was also the makeshift incendiary device or slow-burning fuse, using a cardboard book of matches, of the sort favoured by cheesy nitespots called *Rockerfellers*. The main problem here is getting a cardboard match to strike without detaching it from the book; if you could, you were guaranteed a pretty intense burst of flame for a good twenty seconds – more than enough to melt the flesh on your Action Man or for an anti-fur protester to damage the stock at the Co-Op Drapery.

A duller but much more painful stunt was to try and burn the whole match. This involved holding on to the lit match between the very tip of thumb and forefinger and allowing the match to burn until your nails began to throb and discolour; then grabbing the recently frazzled and still extremely hot end with your other hand so that the flame consumed the whole match, and turned it into the kind of twisted black twig which Tom ends up holding, after Jerry has sabotaged his dynamite.

Then there is the simple but spectacular match-twist, which requires you to hold the match at right-angles to the sandpaper on the box; press hard and twist it back and forth, causing the match head to spark and pop, throwing out splinters of red-hot phosphorus, mainly on to the fleshy bit between your thumb and forefinger.

There is no outcome of the combination of boy and matches that does not end in pain.

Outdoor Games

We are talking sport here, because obviously, far more important than staying indoors playing Yahtzee or Cribbage is to go outside and get some fresh air.

'Go on, you'll miss the best of the day!' was the cry of mums across the land. Forty years ago it was quite common for parents to shove us out the door at ten in the morning and for us not to come back until five. Does that sound like such a brilliant childhood? I'm not so sure. Anyway, sport is what makes a boy manly and there is clearly an approved list of proper ways for a lad to work up a sweat. Predictably, though, the ones dearest to the publishers of *The Boys' Own Book of Fun* (and the like) tend to have a bit of a, well, posh feel to them.

Tennis

You can say what you like about tennis …. no, really you can because I'll probably agree with it. It's a poncey game for overwrought, spoilt and pampered kids. If any of them show the slightest hint of talent they end up being driven miles around the country by their pushy parents to appallingly snooty tournaments where everyone is banging on about getting 'the right coach'. Any game where you have to have your own personal coach has to be a bit suspect. They hardly spend any time on teaching kids how to actually play tennis – it's all that psychological crap about the game being in the mind and 'centring one's self in the zone'. In some cases, particularly with girl tennis players, the coach is also their certifiably barmy control-freak of a father. Some successful women tennis players have had to have restraining orders placed on their loony dads to keep them away from them. The chances of anyone playing a lot of tennis and not developing some kind of personality disorder are pretty remote.

Look at this list – you've got the androids Borg, Sampras and Henman and the brattish Andy Murray; Rafa Nadal with his stupid shorts-hitching and Roger Federer with his own monogrammed pyjamas. The only tennis player who seems remotely bearable is McEnroe, but only since he gave the game up. Before that he was an insufferable twat.

You may argue that there are plenty of ordinary people innocently knocking tennis balls around their municipal concrete courts on sunny summer's evenings, but if you happen to be strolling by one of these courts, have a listen to the barely subdued aggression bubbling up under the Fred Perrys and the cricket sweaters. Like squash, tennis is the kind of game played by men who like to think of themselves as 'alpha-males', grunting and sweating and expressing their hatred for one another through pummelled tennis balls and abused racquets. These are the people who come up behind you in the fast lane and flash you to move aside when *you're* doing 85 already.

Of course, tennis is a rich person's game and all the rivalry is expressed in the proper competitive spirit; some rather embarrasing fist-pumping, yes, but no rough stuff or oikish behaviour. When did you last hear of a tennis player coming from the ranks of the great unwashed? 'Oh yes, he was taken from the slums in the backstreets – his raw talent spotted when he was playing tennis with a frying pan and some rolled-up newspaper.' It just doesn't happen. Fred Perry is one of the few examples of a working-class player making it to the top but his dad was an MP so you could hardly call his a normal upbringing.

Did I forget to mention any other crap things about tennis? Oh yes, the silly hair, the stupid baseball caps and visors and bandanas and shirts that are specially designed to fly up during a match to show off the torso. And of course, the clincher – just remind yourself of this almost-forgotten cry any time someone tries to persuade you to watch or play tennis at any level – 'Come on, Tim!'

Rugby

If golf is a good walk spoiled, then rugby is a fight near an egg-shaped ball. And yet, playing rugby is somehow supposed to have helped build the English character. All the major public schools force it on their pupils because it's deemed to have such a beneficial effect on the rude health and mental well-being of young boys. Odd, then, that almost all grown-up rugby players feel obliged to put on suspenders and dress up as women at the slightest opportunity. When I was at college it was often hard to recognise rugby players when they weren't wearing their make-up. It's also odd that the further down the posh-school ladder you go, the more real rugby fanatics you find. This is so that a lowly school's reputation can be enhanced by 'beating the toffs at their own game'. At my state school in the mid-70s, we were surrounded by four major rugby league clubs (Wakefield, Castleford, Leeds and Featherstone) and the greatest football team in Europe at the time, Leeds United, and yet we were forced to play rugby union against the local grammars and private schools to help the headmaster alleviate the discomfort of the chip on his shoulder.

Wholesome Entertainment

The game of rugby was invented, so the story goes in 1823. William Webb Ellis was at Rugby School playing football or, as posh people call it, footer, and he picked up the ball and ran with it and invented the game which is now called rugby or, if you're a posh person, rugger. What a shame he didn't go to Dulwich College; then we could call it 'duller'.

It is, in fact, highly unlikely that Webb Ellis invented the game simply by catching a football (allowed) and running with it (not allowed) because surely everyone would have stopped, looked at him and shouted, 'Oi, Ellis, you wanker, what the hell are you playing at?' or more likely, 'I say there, Ellis, you scoundrel, what the deuce do you think you're doing? Free kick, sir!' And if he didn't stop surely he would have the shit kicked out of him.

Funnily enough, the legality of kicking the shit out of each other is what actually caused the split between football and rugby. 'Hacking' or kicking an opponent on the shins was allowed in rugby but frowned upon in football, and eventually disappeared from the game altogether in 2003 when Wimbledon F. C. went bust.

To be honest, no-one knows what the rules of rugby union are. They are ridiculously incomprehensible and they change from one game to the next so that no one knows what's meant to be going on. The only consistent rule seems to be that the referee will blow his whistle at random throughout the game and award penalties to one side or the other. These are kicked and missed or kicked and scored – it's impossible to tell either way because there's no net and no crossbar – then the game is over and everyone can receive medical treatment. Ironically, given the mythical origins of the game, picking the ball up and running with it is almost unheard of today.

There was a point when skinny men like Gerald Davies, David Duckham and Grant Batty would skip around hulking great forwards for a thrilling try, and there'd be breathtaking sequences of passing ('Pullen, John Dawes, Davey – Tom Davey, Quinnell – this is Gareth Edwards – what a score!'[1]), but now everyone is 25 stone and can run and tackle and consequently no one does anything except kick and push.

Maybe I'm romanticising. Of course I am. As a kid watching the Five Nations I couldn't wait to play a proper game of rugby when I got to secondary school, but then I found out first-hand what an utterly stupid, dangerous game for complete dunderheads it is. Wintergreen oil, scrum pox, ripped ears, gouged eyes, broken collarbones, busted noses – these are the true marks of rugby. And this is not to mention the social scars. There is an old joke trotted out by devotees of 'the oval ball' – rugby is a ruffian's game played by gentlemen, whereas football is a gentleman's game played by ruffians. How I've laughed on the hundred-odd occasions I've endured that joke following some footballing outrage or tragedy. But the infuriating fact is, it's partly true – football originated in the top public schools and was codified by Cambridge undergraduates. And rugby is indeed a ruffian's game, but it's played by arseholes, not gentlemen.

Go into any London pub on a Saturday afternoon when the rugby is on and you will not be able to move for baseball-hatted Tobys and their lantern-jawed girlfriends braying at the big screen and breaking into mystifying choruses of 'Swing Low Sweet Chariot'. Of course there won't be any real violence, like

---

[1] Barbicans v All Blacks, 1973

there might be after a televised football match, but somewhere in the vicinity, later on in the evening when the jugs of ale have been downed, some of these rugger buggers will be committing the most heinous crimes such as dropping trousers, dangling bollocks into pints, wearing traffic cones and, yes, dressing up as women. In short, behaving like they were still students, which like the sin of blasphemy against the Holy Spirit, is unforgiveable.

If you must know what the rules of rugby union are, or what some of the terminology means, here is a completely incomplete glossary:

Scrum-half – gets the ball out of the scrum then passes it. That's it.

Fly-half – used to be stand off-ish

Hooker – what most rugby players like to dress up as at parties

Ruck – a lot of big repressed homosexuals piling on top of one another

Maul – ditto

Bind – having to watch rugby with someone who likes it

Flanker – rhyming slang

Loosehead - a common injury

Right wing – most rugby people are

2nd-Phase ball – someone's dropped it and they don't know what to do

Line-out – any players that feel like it lift each other in the air for no reason

Knock on – illegal forward motion of ball, banned in case it leads to anything interesting happening

Offside – standing anywhere on pitch while the game is in progress and mussels are in season

Forward pass – passing the ball forwards. An ancient rule that is largely ignored.

Crossing over – deciding rugby league is a better game

Try – to imagine someone actually running with the ball.

Cricket

In a completely laudable introduction to its section on cricket, *The Dangerous Book For Boys* declares:

There are few better ways of spending a summer than learning to play cricket

But I challenge the notion that you can learn to play cricket in one summer. Cricket is just not a natural game; bowling with a straight arm, batting with your elbow high – these are things you have to be taught for years by a games teacher with brilliantined hair, a pipe and a pencil moustache. I am nearly fifty and I still hold a bat horizontally. I may be from Yorkshire and I'm sure cricket should be in my genes but I am totally useless. I didn't invent the long-hop but I have perfected it and I tend not to take many catches because that ball bloody hurts!

And while we're on the subject of avoiding pain and injury, look at the padding you are supposed to wear to prevent the corky from cracking your bones – thigh-pad, elbow-pad, leg-pad, shoulder-pad, helmet, gloves, box. It's longer than the roll call for the Trumpton fire brigade.

Most casual footballers could struggle through a game of Sunday football without embarrassing themselves too much, but put an uninitiated person onto a cricket field when it's eleven against eleven and they'll be more out of place than Abu Hamza in a juggling contest.

The fate of anyone who can be trusted with neither bat nor ball, nor close-fielding, is to be banished to the farthest reaches of Long Off or Third Man for the best part of five hours, with only the occasional embarrassment of a dropped catch in prospect.

But why do people get so misty-eyed about cricket? What is its hold over the British, or rather English, psyche? Why is it deemed to be so good for building character? How many more questions can I squeeze into this paragraph?

Well, like all things to do with Britain – class is at the root of it. Despite the existence of all the Boycotts, Truemans, Flintoffs, Collingwoods, Tuffnells, Bothams and Goughs, cricket is a posh person's game. In addition to hours of coaching, you need a huge amount of land and expensive kit to play cricket – the sort of things you find at large country houses or public schools. This is the world people have in mind when they idealise cricket. A *Famous Five/Jeeves and Wooster* kind of world with long holidays, a private wood to build your tree house in and annual cricket matches between The House and The Village.

Fair enough – it sounds brilliant and who wouldn't want to

live that kind of life? Many many more than the 0.1 per cent of the population who actually achieve it. Its values are not to be sniffed at – fair play, respect for tradition and gentlemanly behaviour – and all these are supposed to be embodied in the game of cricket. Sadly, none of that is true.

One of the more appallingly snobbish aspects of cricket has been the division between 'gentlemen' (amateurs) and 'players' (professionals). It was only abolished in 1963, would you believe, and totally stigmatised professional cricketers as grubby tradesmen. The moral superiority of the 'gentlemen' was enshrined in the rules of matches between the two groups, which allowed the captain of the 'gentlemen' to overrule the umpire if they thought his decisions looked a bit 'shabby'. Overruling or questioning the umpire has been the norm for years now; everyone tampers with the ball and batsmen refuse to walk unless they can see themselves undone on a super slo-mo camera.

You can add to this the air of uncertainty and mistrust which hangs over every game since match-rigging by the big gambling syndicates appeared on the scene, leading great players like Hansie Cronje to sell his birthright for a leather jacket. The phrase 'it's not cricket' would surely not have arisen if the game hadn't been full of cheats.

But what about the quintessential Englishness of cricket and its respect for traditions going back hundreds of years? After all, this is the game which, according to Lord Harris, once the secretary of the MCC, has 'done more to consolidate the Empire than any other influence'. Well, it seems that cricket may well have been invented, not in England, but in Belgium. Yes, Belgium. I have a sneaking regard for the much-maligned

Belgians. Beer, chips, salad cream, brilliant art, Tintin and more museums per head of population than anywhere else in the world – what a contribution to civilisation! And one to which we can probably add the invention of cricket, thanks to a group of Flemish weavers throwing a ball (bal) at a stool (stomp) and trying to hit the ball with a curved stick (krik) in the sixteenth century. Chased out of the Low Countries in the Thirty Years War, these cottage industrialists settled on the big estates of Essex, Kent and Sussex to become the inspiration for generations of English toffs.

So, to sum up, cricket is an unnatural, slightly snobbish game, full of cheats and invented by foreigners.

Golf

I have no problem with older men taking up golf as a way of keeping fit and testing their skill, but for a growing boy to be striding around a golf course when he could be slumped on a sofa playing video games is almost criminal. My dad tried to get me to take golf up when I was eleven. This was before computer games, but thank God there was *Scooby Doo* and *The Harlem Globetrotters* and *The Banana Splits* to keep me indoors. I think my dad only wanted me to start playing so that I could make money when I was older. In fact he was pretty open about it – 'by the time you're twenty you can keep me in the lap of luxury'. He may well have been right – I would have had the field to myself. There were no young golfers anywhere on TV in the 70s, or any golfer that looked young. For all I know, Tony Jacklin might have been a teenager when he won the British Open; people looked so *old* in those days. Bobby Charlton was only 29 when he won the World Cup and he looked about 100.

I've only heard one good argument for playing golf before

retirement age and that was from an extremely competitive friend who began playing in his thirties so he would be better than everyone else at 65 when they had all stopped working. His cunning plan did not take into account that, the way the pensions system is going, people will still be grafting well into their eighties and he'll have no-one to play with.

Even as an eighty-year-old I would have to draw the line at golf's compulsory fashion crimes. It seems no-one is allowed on the course unless they have handed their dignity in at the clubhouse and selected their outfit from Jonathan Ross's charity bin-bag. And feeble eighty-year-old though I might be, it would be difficult to prevent myself throttling anyone who shouted 'get in the hole!' after teeing off.

Football

Funny how playing football is never really welcomed into the approved list of proper ways for a boy to enjoy himself. You suspect that it's seen as just a little bit grubby, a bit pikey, a bit urban, even? I wouldn't ever be so stupid as to call it The Beautiful Game – that's about as appropriate as calling a Member of Parliament honourable. Yes, there is cheating, spitting, diving, fouling, abusing officials and rampant greed but I look at football like a good sketch show on TV. There'll be five minutes of some unforgiveable rubbish, but you know within a few seconds something brilliant will happen – unless it's Horne and Corden. Obviously there are dangers in football. You could be beaten or stabbed to death by rival supporters, you could be crushed to death in an overcrowded stadium, or you could become a successful premier league footballer and, every day of your pampered life, die a little inside. Your WAG might lure you into setting up in a £10 million mansion somewhere in Cheshire with the floorspace of an out-of-town Tesco and the style to match; you may be tempted to splash out on a Baby Bentley with white leather seats, darkened windows and a big neon sign on the roof that says 'dickhead', and you may find yourself in an unseemly bout of slapping and pushing in a cheesy nightclub, shouting out to anyone who'll listen: 'Don't you know who I am?'

Snooker

Now here is a proper game albeit not strictly an outdoor one. I can think of no better way for a young man to spend the long, hot summer afternoons than in a cool, dark, air-conditioned snooker club. There's usually toasted sandwiches and beer within easy reach and the only sound to disturb the tranquillity is the occasional high-velocity potting of a red in the corner pocket, or the mutterings of Chinese waiters gambling their wages away.

The appeal of snooker has to be the colours; even a child can enjoy them. Watching snooker is like observing a very fast-moving game of Cluedo, er, with a lot of Miss Scarletts. And there are only two things you have to do in snooker. One is pot a ball, the other is stop your opponent from potting one. It's warm, dry, safe and you are unlikely ever to get injured unless you meet Alex Higgins in a mood.

Snooker's greatest exponents provide sound and admirable role models for young men (see Cliff Thorburn p165) and are living proof that anyone can learn to play, even people with glasses (Dennis Taylor). Some people will argue that snooker's no different from tennis or golf in that you need expensive equipment and hours and hours of practice to be any good and only wealthy people can afford their own snooker tables. That would explain, then, the presence of all those posh snooker players like Ronnie O'Sullivan, Steve Davis, Jimmy White and Ray Reardon.

There are others who will complain that snooker isn't a sport at all – you don't have to be fit to do it. Rubbish. Most snooker players are whippet-thin, underweight if anything and, yes, a bit pasty-faced but when did you ever see a fat snooker player? Apart from, of course, the excellent Bill Werbeniuk (RIP, he's dead *and* tore his trousers in the World Championshps). But Bill wasn't fat because he was lazy, or because snooker didn't give him enough exercise: he needed twenty pints of lager a day to stop his cue arm shaking. It was a genuine medical condition accepted by the game's governing body – Bill needed about eight pints before he could begin a session then and a pint per frame to keep him going. Someone told him to stop drinking because of his health so he had to take a beta-blocker to stop the arm tremor, which was then declared an illegal substance and Bill had to retire. I think there's a lesson for us all there.

Bowls

Another excellent game! Of course, I'm not talking about ten pin bowling – that's fun for about ten minutes once you've got over the unpleasantness of putting on someone else's smelly shoes that are only fumigated with a quick aerosol spray. When you've managed to get the bowling ball from one end of the alley to the other there is some sense of achievement but after that it's all pretty monotonous. You get a strike or you don't, and if you don't, you lose. It's like basketball – you don't get your shot in the hoop, the other team goes up their end and scores.

No – I'm talking crown green bowling, which is a far superior game altogether. The fact that it is played almost exclusively by old men in caps is one of the chief reasons to recommend it. Everyone ages about two decades when they step on to a bowling green. You'd think the Nostalgia Police would be urging everyone to take up bowls: it's about as close as you can get to the 1950s without visiting the Isle of Wight. And when did you ever see an overtly competitive, flash young bowls player? The only way you could sustain an injury in crown green bowls is if you inadvertently got your finger trapped between another man's balls, and that never, ever happens on a bowling green. In daylight.

Toys and the Fascism of Wood

The aversion to plastic by the advocates of wooden toys (and the Proper Childhood Police) is bordering on the racist – or should I say materialist? Take a look at some of the bigotry in the catalogues promoting wooden toys both on the internet and in the parenting press – it's verging on hate crime.

Apparently, compared to wood, plastic makes you stupid:

Studies show that children who play with wooden toys are often better at solving problems. This kind of imaginative play in early childhood provides a solid foundation for later academic learning.

Imagine how stupid the Chinese must be, surrounded by all those plastic toys?

Then, of course, there's the aesthetic appeal:

Ask yourself this … would you prefer to sit at a chunky solid oak table or a plastic alternative with a cold and shiny veneer top?

Damn that cold and shiny veneer! It appears that plastic is 'evil' too – it gives off chemicals, it can split and splinter causing sharp edges and the colours are crude and garish. The overall verdict then, on plastic, is don't let it near your daughter.

The truth is, unless the toy is a cricket bat, or a xylophone, a plastic one is always better. Take marble runs – have you seen the ingenuity of the plastic ones? All those curves and spirals and beautiful colours! Wooden marble runs go in straight lines and the holes never match up. Then there's Duplo, LEGO, Airfix Kits (see below), *Star Wars* figures, Action Men, Nurf Guns, radio-controlled tanks, helicopters, Robosapiens, Rubik's Cube, Subbuteo, Micro Stars: you name it, plastic is best. And a child knows he has a toy in his hands and not just something that will blend in with his parents' interior design scheme.

'But wood is biodegradable!' cry the materialists – yes, and so is a forest, but it's going to be around for a bloody long time. I'll bet my plastic Buzz Lightyear toy is being put to good use, by being recycled as part of a waterproof roof-covering on *Grand Designs*, years before your set of wooden building blocks has been broken down into pulp by successive generations of beetles. And anyway, if we want to take all the carbon out of the atmosphere and back into fossil fuel, the best thing we can do with plastic is bury it in landfill sites. Problem solved.

Airfix and Meccano

We now enter into the strange twilight world between the spectral gloom of the Nintendo addict and the bright, clean, fresh air of the wood-whittlers. A land where nothing is certain, where ingenuity, ruggedness, dexterity, science, technology, courage, craftsmanship, heartiness and nerditude all swirl together and no one can tell good from evil.

This is the land of Airfix and Meccano; possibly the two best toys ever invented. They simultaneously stimulate and destroy imagination and creativity; they are a blast from the past and a rocket to the future. They're for wimps and real men; they are tradition and transience, for the nimble-fingered and the brain dead.

The High Priest of Airfix and Meccano is James May. Mocked by the cruel moderns Hammond and Clarkson for being slow and old-fashioned, James May is in fact highly intelligent and technologically savvy. He's just as comfortable with a thought-powered robot as he is with a 1952 Sunbeam S8 600cc parallel twin. If a kid wants a role model, James May is it.

Airfix and Meccano are the quintessence of a traditional British schoolboy's childhood. Look for a Google image of either and you are likely to find a kid in a tank-top with short back and sides reverently holding up a Spitfire or joyfully operating a Meccano scale model of the Middlesbrough Transporter Bridge. Journalists love to contrast the quaintness and innocence of these toys with the knowing sophistication of the Wii generation. And yet, to the lover of the outdoors, the devotee of woodcraft and maker of his own bow and arrow, the Airfix model-makers and Meccano engineers are nothing but pasty-faced, stay-at-home speccy-four-eyes. They are limited by the pieces in the box and can only build by following instructions. But what mighty things they can build! A Flying Fortress, a Sunderland Flying Boat, a tower crane, a motorised jeep, a working windmill and the Red Baron's Fokker Triplane.

I don't think I can wax lyrically enough about the joy that Airfix and Meccano have brought to me and the fact that they fall into neither camp in the great Proper Toy war delights me even more. I am now giddy with the heady aroma of positivity (or is it glue?) and I think I need to lie down.

Why Computer Games Are Brilliant

For some people the computer game is the most evil invention ever to spring out of the mind of man. Forget guns, slavery, capitalism or *The Jeremy Kyle Show* – the PlayStation, the Wii, the DS and the X-Box are the four horsemen of the digital apocalypse. There is an on-line ad for a certain large, red, heavily embossed book about dads and lads doing dangerous things which begins with a crepuscular boy in a dingy bedroom transfixed by a hand-held console. His dad enters the room with the Big Red Book and the next thing you know we are whisked out into a sunny day where father and son are having some real fun.

If I came home and found my sons playing FIFA 09 on the PlayStation my first reaction would be – 'who's winning?' *Isn't that the better world?*

When I was a boy I used to flick my Subbuteo players disconsolately around on my own (my brothers couldn't have been more bored by it) just wishing it was a bit more realistic. I had a sneaking feeling that the ball shouldn't really be bigger than the players themselves: maybe Subbuteo wasn't actually like real football at all? There were a couple of games where you moved the men around by waggling magnets underneath the pitch and then Striker came along! You pressed the player's head down and he actually kicked the ball! The goalies would dive too if you handled them properly. But still I wanted the men to move around the pitch of their own free will – an impossible dream, surely? It was almost ten years before the home computer was able to make my dream come true. International Soccer, Kick Off, EA sports and Pro Evolution Soccer have brought totally realistic-looking footballers into my living room for me to control.

What child of the 1950s, fumbling around with his Subbuteo players on what essentially was an old army blanket, would not weep with joy at the computerised football game? How can it possibly be wrong?

'But why aren't kids out kicking footballs instead of watching little figures do it on screen?' Who says they aren't? Picking up a games console doesn't cast a magic spell which glues you to the floor, just as playing Subbuteo didn't stop me wanting to go outside. And computer games are not just sports simulation. Shoot 'em ups and platform games encourage lightning reactions, quick thinking and problem solving. They stimulate imagination and creativity just as much as a film or TV show would do. And just because there are computer games which are a bad influence on kids, like say Grand Theft Auto, Resident Evil or God of War, doesn't mean they all are, just as the existence of *Texas Chainsaw Massacre* or *Henry Portrait of a Serial Killer* doesn't give you any clue as to the content of *Dr Strangelove* or *A Matter of Life and Death*.

I think the main reason why parents get worked up about kids playing computer games is jealousy. They never had them so why should today's children? Because something is powered by electricity and needs a screen it is automatically a bad thing, while coloured wooden blocks or modelling clay or kites or wigwams or anything that involves fresh air is automatically good. The more kids from the computer-game generation become parents the sooner these games will lose their stigma. My parents couldn't comprehend me leaving the table after Christmas dinner to watch *Top of the Pops*, but now that example of poor table manners and lack of respect for tradition is itself enshrined on TV list shows as grade 1 listed nostalgia.

Young people in their twenties are already nostalgic for Sonic the Hedgehog and Super Mario and in the future, we'll be reading Christmas gift-books that criticise modern youth for being addicted to watching movies on the screen implanted in their retina rather than watching them on their iPhone 'like we used to'.

Sadly, even nostalgia isn't what it used to be these days. In my day we had a *proper* longing for things past. Time was when several generations would share the same hobbies and interests; kids were amusing themselves with a hoop and stick (if they were lucky) for the entire nineteenth century. As recently as the 60s and 70s two decades' worth of children were familiar with John Noakes and able to scoff at the latest set of feeble *Blue Peter* presenters. Nowadays, tastes change every couple of years: today's three-year-olds will have no idea who the Fimbles are; they're so 2002! The new big thing is Waybuloo. Can't we all just accept that things change and not always for the worst (except Action Man and that ridiculous realistic hair and beard).

Non Essential Kit for Boys:

A Magnifying Glass

Not much to say about this. Magnifying glasses make things bigger. Good for reading small print but you'll have plenty of time to do that when you're old. Use your naked eyes while you can.

I suppose you could look at a small insect under a magnifying glass and focus the rays of the sun on the little mite's body until it combusts. But really, sunlight-based insect extermination takes about five minutes in good strong sunlight, and we have that in this country about twice a year. Plus the insect will probably be moving around a lot so it could take you an hour to kill just one bug. Is it really worth the wait? If you're desperate for fun, you could set light to a piece of paper with the magnifying glass, but you've got a box of matches to start a fire, for God's sake.

Chapter Three
Old-fashioned Adventure

We're getting down to the hardcore stuff now. This section deals with all the totally insane suggestions, from books like the *Perfectly Ripping Book of Larks* (See bibliography), for ways to risk your life outside the home. Most of them require you to encounter people/animals/fire/water/rope in ways any sane person would, y'know, rather not.

We're approaching a strange territory where several worlds collide: the world of all those books, which have jumped on the Proper Childhood Police bandwagon, and what they would call 'harmlessly frittering away a summer afternoon'; the world of those slightly potty survivalist experts who think every boy should know how to dig a snow-hole and survive on the wildlife he can kill (and I include Hugh Fearnley-Whittingstall in this); and the world of those people who believe in physical strength, endurance, and being equipped for the day when 'It All Kicks Off', i.e. the Scout Movement. Be Prepared. Be very prepared.

• • • • • • • • • • • •

Lurking

• •

One of the activities that *Boys Books of Everything*, claim to be so exciting is 'spying on people' – lurking around corners, peeping through holes in newspapers, noting down movements, taking photographs. Actually, these days this is less like 'spying' and more like 'working for the council'. *The Spiffing Book of Spycraft* should probably have chapters in it on 'monitoring the level of recyclable material in your neighbour's bins' and 'checking that the posh couple aren't just renting in your area to get into the local grammar school'.

Playing at spies is indeed great fun. Running around the house, walking backwards into rooms like Robert Vaughn, carrying toy guns with silencers and trying to talk with an American accent are perfectly acceptable.

But that's as far as it should go.

There are some books, however, which would have ten-year-old boys trained and tooled-up like a child soldier from Chad. And no matter how many health warnings are printed in those books that try to interest kids in spookery, items like 'How to Pursue Someone on Top of a Train' are bound to inspire the wrong kind of role play in some warped personalities. Train surfing is, just so you know, killing quite large numbers of young people in places like Brazil and South Africa.

OK, let's not get hung up on a casual throw-away reference to suicidal practices on the roof of a Pendolino. Here are some of the less extreme but none the less dicey activities in the world of juvenile espionage ....

Tailing and Snooping

There's a campaign currently gaining momentum in the UK called 'Guerilla Geography' which, among other things, advocates that kids should travel further and further away from home than they do now. One guerilla geographer (imagine that on your business card) actually made a speech at a conference in which he said, rather controversially, that more children must die to make the rest of them more adventurous. I'd love to see that on an election manifesto.

Guerilla Geography suggests an unusual way of tempting children to stray out of their neighbourhood – following someone at random for an hour to see where it leads them. It recommends using the old 'eyeholes in the magazine' trick, but adds a priceless caveat – 'when shadowing or spying on a person through the holes in your magazine, make sure the person you are following is not a meany'. Well, that's one way of advising caution. And how do you find out if he is a meany? At what point do you discover this – when the doors slam on the transit van as you are driven off?

As kids, my brothers and I decided to spy on a local character we thought was dodgy and mysterious. He was a cobbler we rather imaginatively called 'Cobby'. We had convinced ourselves that because he had a hump and a three-wheeler disabled carriage, he was up to no good. That's the 1960s for you.

Good Old-fashioned Adventure

One morning, we sneaked out of bed early to discover which direction he trundled in from. When we had figured that out, we got up again the next day, and the next – gradually tracing his journey back to his house by a process of elimination. This made us extremely tired and rubbish at school. Sneaking out of the house while your parents are still asleep is always in Enid Blyton books – it is often a rather stupid and inefficient method of finding something out compared to just asking your parents – 'Er, Mum, where does the cobbler with the hunchback live … and is he a criminal?' That way we'd have avoided a lot of unnecessary effort, tiredness, poor performance in school tests and a visit from the local police for 'worrying a cripple'.

The other annoying aspect of this sort of tailing is that it's so old-fashioned. Modern surveillance involves simply slapping a tracking device on the suspect's car or briefcase and following the moving dot on one of those big screens as it goes 'bleep-bleep'. Or in the case of the Metropolitan Police, following the wrong bloke into a tube station and shooting him seven times in the head.

I've always been far more attracted by the art of 'shaking *off* a tail'– losing someone who's following you. This is clearly

rooted in self-preservation and designed to get you out of danger, not land you in it. I always wanted to try the James Bond method of shaking off a tail, whereby you stumble across a Mardi Gras parade, heaving with shimmying Brazilian totty. You mingle with the dancers, doing a bit of shimmying yourself with one of the friskier ones, and then duck out on the other side of the street, leaving the bull-necked assassin struggling to get through the crowd (he's not nearly as light on his feet as you) as the jovial revellers knock off his trilby. Actually, come to think of it, this scene happens in pretty much every spy movie, except the ones with Jason Bourne in them.

●●●●●●●●●●●●●●●●●●●

Secret Codes

●●

Secret codes, passwords and hand signals are the sherbet lemons in the child spy's sweet shop. Nice to look at, cleverly made and, er … fizzy, no … bitter. Actually, that metaphor doesn't work. Anyway, they are highly prized.

Proper codes are created and deciphered by mad maths geniuses. Don't even think about doing that. As you may read elsewhere (see page 152) being too good at maths is a huge mistake. And being good at codebreaking-style maths puts you into the Alan Turing category of oddball; not a recipe for a happy life. Yes, OK, he helped us win the war against the Nazis; yes, he paved the way for modern computers; but was he *happy*? More to the point, was he poisoned? The Apple logo is supposed to have a bite out of it to remind us that the inventor of the computer was murdered by a poisoned apple. (Nice thought, chaps.)

But let's remind ourselves of the lesson again – geniuses are never welcome after they've geniused; when they've given us their masterpieces, people tend to go off them in a big way. Take Mozart – he was murdered by the mysterious masked man, wasn't he? Well, he was according to the film. He also apparently had an annoying laugh and talked about farting a lot.

These are borderline-acceptable grounds for poisoning someone, but we still ended up with the music, so well done us. All Mozart got was lingering death and poverty. Look at Daedalus – he built an amazing labyrinth for King Minos and got locked up for his pains, with only his idiot son for company. And there's the tragic case of Nik Kershaw who, despite his undoubted gift for melodic hooks, profound lyrics and virtuoso performances on the guitar-shaped keyboard, is rudely mocked as a jump-suited dwarf with a silly haircut.

In the same way, genius kids are neither welcomed nor loved by society – their glasses are stolen, their ears are flicked, they are tripped in the playground and their satchels are filled with excrement. A great friend of mine from school was a precociously talented artist, but the bullies would corner him in the cloakroom and force him to draw porn – 'Draw us a naked woman or I'll smack thee.' Fortunately he was always drawing naked women anyway, so it wasn't much of an imposition. But a naked woman with a dog … well, he had to draw the line somewhere.

Anyway, back to codes. All codes are dangerous to start with because they actually *attract* attention – no self-respecting baddie prince is going to look at a weird jumble of letters and numbers and think, 'That's strange, I can't understand all these symbols. Never mind, it's probably nothing. It's addressed to the head of my armed forces so I'd best let him read it.'

The serious codemakers know their messages will be intercepted so just concentrate on making them as stupefyingly difficult as possible. But these serious, proper codes are no fun at all. The Enigma Machine, in Bletchley, despite its important place in history, loses me completely at the bit where wheels rotate with every keystroke and every character operates on a different code sys… *zzzzzzzzz.*

But it's the smugness of these cryptographers that really gets up my pipe. And there are more of them about than you think. You can see them finishing the *Observer* crossword in offensively quick time (I know the *Observer* crossword isn't that difficult; *you're* just the kind of smug bastard I'm talking about).

Easy codes on the other hand are just that – easy and rubbish. A=1 B=2; or A=Z and B=Y. These substitution codes are probably quite effective because it's so laughably easy to decipher them that you give up with boredom after you've read MEET ME IN THE LANGUAGE LABS, before you get to the bit where it says it's from Jacqueline Tilley in 5S.

Morse Code

Samuel Morse invented his ingenious system of dots and dashes to work both visually and audibly. You can use almost anything to send Morse signals. I tried it once by whacking a tree with a big stick, but it sounded like the beat to 'Blue Monday' by New Order.

My dad was a telegraphist air gunner in World War Two and could use Morse code at a phenomenal speed, but I know he was delighted when they brought radio in and he would have jumped at the chance to send text-messages – of course he would, he was only nineteen at the time.

So why do people think Morse is still worth learning? – it's about as difficult as ancient Greek. At the beginning of 2009, furious correspondents to newspapers like the *Daily Telegraph* were complaining that the Scouts were introducing a Texting Badge. But why shouldn't they? Just because it's a modern invention that requires electricity? The great assault on texting led by grumpy newspaper columnists completely ignores the fact that most people sending text messages are adults and that young people only abbreviate the words because it's cool to do so; not because they don't know how to spell them. Morse code has served its purpose and I'm proud of my nineteen-year-old dad for being so good at it, but for me the only useful demonstration of Morse code in the last twenty years has been in the soundtrack composition of Barrington Pheloung, who used it to spell out the name of the killer in code throughout every episode of *Inspector Morse*.

Flag Signals

Another old-fashioned form of communication that although still used for some signals at sea is basically held in awe by lovers of 'the old ways' because of Lord Nelson. Famously Nelson sent the signal 'England Expects That Every Man Will Do His Duty'. This has been taken as the stirring rallying cry to be trotted out on every occasion demanding a patriotic response, and sometimes by idiot newspaper editors on the eve of football matches. Actually Nelson only sent that message because he didn't have enough flags to send 'Nelson Confides (i.e. is confident) That Every Man Will Do His Duty' – a little bit less stern, quite cool in fact, but also a little bit arrogant on behalf of the old one-eyed, one-armed bighead. It doesn't really detract from the man's genius or the heroism of the men at Trafalgar, but what it does demonstrate is how useless sending signals is. The word 'expects' was in the naval code-book and had its own signal. However, 'confides' needed spelling out letter by letter.

In the heat of the moment you need to be able to get your message across quickly and maybe children today, rather than be told about Nelson's flag signals, should take as their inspiration the modern equivalent of 'England Expects' – the 9/11 rallying cry from Todd Beamer on Flight 93, overheard on a mobile phone, 'Let's Roll!'

The Skytale

Perhaps the most ridiculous code that spying books recommend to children is the *skytale* (rhymes with Italy). It was used by the Spartans to pass secret messages to each other on the battlefield, but it worked in those days because a *skytale* is a wooden military baton, quite commonly used by the Spartans who did little else but clout recruits on the head with it. The message was written on a thin strip of paper wound around the baton in a spiral and could only be decoded on a baton of a similar size. No-one in 480BC would suspect a Spartan carrying a big stick. But these days you can't casually tote a two-foot-long stick into double French class and sneak a secret message to Jacqueline Tilley – who would also have to be in possession of similarly sized baton to decode your offer of a tryst – and hope to get away with it.

The Tattooed Head

One of the weirdest secret messages ever sent side-stepped the whole code/substitution business, and even the authors of books such as *Go On, Climb A Tree, It's Worth The Broken Leg*, wouldn't think of including it in a list of suggestions to while away the afternoon. It's from Herodotus, the Greek historian who listened to a lot of stuff that probably wasn't true but printed it anyway – a kind of fifth century BC Piers Morgan. It's the story of Histiaeus who wanted to instigate a revolt against the Persians on the island of Miletus, so he shaved his most trusted slave's head and had the word 'revolt' tattooed on his bald scalp. He then waited for the hair to grow back and sent the slave to his ally the tyrant of Miletus, with a message saying 'this slave needs a haircut'. It's a great story but, like all secret messages, it's way more trouble than it's worth and not particularly secret. I can't imagine a tyrant would have been bothered to shave a slave's head himself; they are not renowned for their patience, tyrants; so other people must have seen the message before he did. Why didn't Histiaeus just write 'revolt' on the piece of paper instead of 'this slave needs a haircut'? The job could have been done in half the time. Writing words on to people's shaven heads never really caught on as a way of inciting rebellion, although it has resurfaced on the heads of small children in some parts of Britain as a way of promoting certain brands of sportswear.

Invisible Ink

So simple, isn't it? All you need is a quill pen and some lemon juice. Now I'm sure we had a quill pen and some lemon juice somewhere ... actually, in the post-Jamie Oliver era, when the entire population has been converted to making 'proper fakkin' larvely fakkin' jablee food', everyone has litres of spare lemon juice in the house. When I grew up in the early sixties, the only approximation to lemon juice was PLJ – an ultra-concentrated lemon extract that would burn a hole through Time itself if you let it out of the bottle. But a quill pen? Where the hell was I meant to get a quill pen?! *The fifteenth century?!*

Luckily for me, there was a proper nib – on my dad's 1930s geometry set. So I used that to scratch some unintelligible rubbish in lemon juice on a piece of cartridge paper, going as fast as I could before the PLJ rotted the nib. Even if I'd used real ink you couldn't have made sense of it. To make the writing appear, I then held it in front of the fire until my knuckles began to blister and proudly showed my brother.

'All I can read is "this",' he said. 'What is it supposed to say?'

It was supposed to say, 'Can you read this?'

And there you have, in a nutshell, the utter pointlessness of invisible ink.[1]

---

[1] You have been spared the obvious joke of just leaving a blank page for this entry.

Tracking and Hunting

Codes, surveillance and tailing people come together in an almost orgasmic rush with these most authentic of all 'dangerous' activities. Tracking animals is one of those skills we all used to have before people invented cars and houses, and the advocates of 'proper fun' and 'healthy outdoor activity', lament its passing deeply. Because of our soft city-dwelling ways we have lost the ability to stand on a hillside, sniff the air and say, 'five horses, heading west, one has lost a shoe, another has very bad wind'.

So we are encouraged to reconnect with nature by trudging around the kind of muddy fields you once encountered only on a compulsory cross-country run, in the hope of spotting some animal tracks that might alert you to the nearby presence of a deer, a badger or a fox. I live in the city and I'm alerted to the presence of foxes by treading in the evil-smelling semi-liquid shit that they deposit by my dustbins most nights, so I don't need to go looking for their footprints.

In the 60s and 70s people were so concerned about a young person's ability to follow animal tracks in the countryside that they harnessed the power of the mighty shoe industry to help. Wayfinders were the shoes that blazed the trail, so to speak, with their animal-track sole. Ten miniature animal prints were moulded on to the bottom of each shoe so you could stamp your foot in the snow (it snowed a lot back in those days) and check the animal tracks you were following against your shoe-guide. But if anyone was actually trying to find *you* when you'd got lost in the wood tracking badgers, they might think they were following a gang of tiny one-legged woodland creatures. Your only hope of getting home alive rested on the tiny compass that the ingenious Wayfinders had secreted in the heel of the shoe.

Now at this point some older readers may be saying to themselves – 'hang on … animal tracks on the soles of shoes … a compass in the heel? Surely they were Clark's Commandos shoes?' Ah yes, Clark's Commandos … whenever anyone starts to reminisce about Spangles and says, 'Do you remember Aztec bars?' and 'Wasn't *Thunderbirds* brilliant?' it's only a matter of time before someone asks if you ever had a pair of Clark's Commandos with the compass in the heel. Several piss-poor comedians have developed twenty-minute stand-up routines on the utter impracticality of putting a compass in the heel of a shoe – ('A compass in the heel? What's that all about? You'd fall over trying to look at it etc') but what is really annoying about this particular piece of nostalgia is that it's totally inaccurate. Clark's Commandos did not have a compass in the heel – those shoes were Wayfinders.

Clark's Commandos had a yellow 'C' on the heel and the shoes came in an army-style ammunition box. Wayfinders had the compass, the animal-print soles, the lunar-surface soles, the lot. Clearly the branding on their advertising was terrible. If, in war, the first casualty is truth then I'm afraid the truth of who had the compass in the heel has been lost in the Crap Shoe Wars of the early 70s.

It's amazing to think that big shoe manufacturers would fight so hard to persuade children to choose *their* particular brand of synthetic leatherette school-approved footwear. Although younger readers will recognise the phenomenon in the Crap

Newspaper Wars of the early 2000s, when the *Guardian* and the *Independent* tried to boost their circulations by printing wall-charts of mushrooms and salad-leaves.

Anyway, suppose I have outgrown my Wayfinders shoes and I am somehow lured into the countryside to scour a muddy woodland path for animal prints, what am I looking for exactly?

Well this is a badger print:

Looks pretty much like a generic animal foot to me but apparently the giveaway is the extended claw. Badgers have sharp claws and teeth and extremely thick skulls; quite extraordinarily thick it seems, and they can be extremely vicious when cornered. I have no intention of ever cornering a badger but apparently the most dangerous thing you can do, according to the West Cornwall Badger group, is attempt to rescue one that's been hit by a car. Badgers can appear to be dead, when only unconscious (it's the thick skull, you see), and can spring awake at a moment's notice. So if, in your compassion, you pick up a comatose badger in the road and place it gently in your car, then rush it to the nearest Badger sanctuary, be prepared; it may spring awake and rip your neck to shreds as you're doing 65mph down the A30.

Here is another spiky hand-type print:

It's an otter apparently. Now, I do like a good otter, particularly when they swim on their backs eating fish. But I'm happy to enjoy my otters on one of the many beautifully shot wildlife films that everyone pays the licence fee for.

I'm sure we all remember what the otter's distant relative the ferret did to Richard Whiteley's finger on national television, don't we? What do you mean 'no'? Well, he was handling a ferret, as you have to do in the north at some point in your life, and it sank its teeth into his index-finger bone.

So, I don't particularly want to encounter one in the wild, especially as my dad once told me that an otter can bite through steel. He might have been making that up to fool me. He often did that, with great success – most notably when he convinced me that the reason Basil D'Oliveira wasn't allowed to play cricket for England in South Africa in 1968 was because he was a woman. But would you believe I went on an otter chat room (yes, they do exist) and it's true! An otter once bit through a man's steel toecap. So there you are – well – done, Dad! My shunning of otters is vindicated.

This next one is a deer.

It's obvious to anyone, apparently, and is the classic example of the cloven hoof. And the cloven hoof means only one thing – the Devil. Yes, the deer is the devil's spawn and you only have to look closely at the imprint of the hoof to see two hooded Ku Klux Klan-type figures with no faces. Actually, by drawing slightly mad faces on the hoof print you can diminish the scary effect, like this:

If you need more evidence as to the satanic nature of the deer, just take a good look at a herd of them in somewhere like Richmond Park. They lurk under trees staring at you with their big scary black eyes and creepy little horns poking out of their heads, eeuuurgh, and how many times have you seen weird pagan village pageants like the Abbots Bromley Horn Dance or that parade in *The Wicker Man* where the chief devil-worshipper has some kind of antler-horn hat? In short, deers are evil. My advice …

Steer clear of deer.

• • • • • • • • • • •
Tramps
• •

If you spend long enough poking around the countryside looking for animal tracks, eventually you'll begin to notice the presence of humans. Now I don't mean cars and houses – that would be ridiculous – I mean the Gentlemen of the Road and their secret code. For over a hundred years, as tramps moved around from place to place, from free meal to free meal, their signs and signals were a series of messages by which tramps let each other know where meals could be had and what trouble to avoid.

Bizarrely, when I was a kid we were encouraged to seek out the secret signs of travellers and follow tramps about, in much the same way as my brothers and I stalked the disabled cobbler in our village (Remember him? Page 88). I suppose in those days a lot of tramps were interesting old coves with intelligence and manners who had fallen on hard times rather than the sweary, ruddy-faced alcoholics or homeless drug addicts of today, but they weren't exactly the kind of company you'd want to seek out, especially as a lot of them carried dozens of knives which they were supposed to be sharpening for people, so why would anyone bother learning the codebook of tramps' secret signals?

Why, indeed, would there be a whole section in the *I-SPY* book of the countryside devoted to tramps' signals and what they mean?

I can only imagine they thought it might be useful to hungry children, lost and in need of a free meal.

This one, above, is meant to be a loaf (not bad, I suppose) and suggests that you might get food handed out to you at the house it has been scrawled upon.

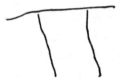

This one is supposed to be a table and suggests you might actually get a sit-down meal. Or it could mean you'll have to calculate the area of a circle before they'll feed you.

Obviously nowadays knocking on the door of a house in the expectation of a sit-down meal would be met with a brief 'fuck off', or if it was Islington, 'I'm sorry, I'm watching the nanny put the children to bed'.

Most likely no one would come to the door at all.

The symbol above on the gate post of a house means 'a Christian family lives here', meaning either you'll be able to guilt-trip them into feeding you or they'll only give you a hot cross bun.

Some social anthropologists think this sign means a 'broken' X and means 'nothing doing at this house', although I think it looks like a corkscrew and probably means 'pissheads live here – fill your boots'.

Finally, this symbol is supposed to warn other tramps that the householder may call the police.

And if there are two of these symbols together, it means the lady of the house often forgets to draw the curtains.

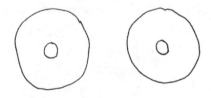

The Scout Movement

It's easy to ignore the importance of the Scout Movement to the British character, for the sake of a few cheap jokes about woggles and bob-a-job week. Easy and funny. In all fairness, though, you can't fault the original motivation of the Scout Movement and its founding fathers. Their moral code underpinned British society for decades in the twentieth century, and the manual *Scouting for Boys* has been extremely influential – it is the Proper Childhood Police's bible.

So what's the problem? Some people say that the uniforms and strict codes of behaviour have fostered a slightly sinister and judgmental organisation. Well, I wouldn't go as far as the trendy teachers of the 1970s who banned Scout activity from schools on the grounds that they were nothing less than paramilitaries, but listen to this tale from the *Scouting For Boys* manual (1908).

It's called 'The Elsdon Murder' and is supposed to show all the best aspects of a Scout in action. A young climber in the hills in Northumberland noticed a grim-looking tramp with hobnail boots sitting by a fence. When he came to a village and found that a woman had been murdered, and he noticed footprints which reminded him of the tramp's boots. He told the police and led them to the tramp who, it turned out, was a gypsy. The tramp was arrested, charged and found guilty, and hanged along with two accomplices. The boy was upset that he had caused the death of a fellow human being but the judge told him to 'never mind about that'.

Now I don't like the idea of murderers getting away with it, but there's a lot of implied trust of authority in that story; a lot of assumptions that gypsy types had guilt written all over them and all observant young Scouts had to do was point them out to the police and all would be well. Were the Scouts intent on creating a nation of snoops and informers?

But actually that is not my big beef with the Scout Movement. The problem with it is embodied in one man, Ben Southall. He's the English chap – and former Scout – who won the so-called 'best job in the world' competition in 2009, to become the caretaker of a stretch of the Great Barrier Reef. Thousands upon thousands of people applied for this job, completely hoodwinked by the totally misleading title. The prize was to live on Hamilton Island, make friends with locals on the Great Barrier Reef and blog about it. So he's on an island which is probably very hot and boring, he has to make friends with people who he won't be able to escape from because he lives on an island, and then blog about it, which, as anyone knows, is the most soul-destroying occupation in the modern world, both for the blogger and anyone who happens across his 'work'.

Apparently of the sixteen final candidates, Ben performed best in the selection tasks of 'snorkelling, swimming, spending time at a spa and at barbecues and blogging'. Can you imagine anything more horrible than that? Well, yes I can, actually – doing all that surrounded by a dozen or so other people who really love doing it too. And how many of those were former Scouts? Er, well, I don't know, but you can see that, despite the high ideals of its founders, the Scout Movement creates people like this. They can abseil, climb, sail, survive in the wild, light fires out of drift-wood, cook food in river water, eat moss, swim in freezing rivers and dry themselves with a handful of leaves, the bastards.

As well as being intensely annoying, all this stuff is genuinely dangerous. How many kids who joined the Scouts as children have been left broken by the wayside through their innate inability to build a campfire by rubbing two sticks together, track an antelope from its droppings and build a raft out of seaweed?

But many young people are still deluded and seduced by the idea of being one of these 'men of the wild', like Bear Grylls or Ray Mears or Bruce Parry or Steve Irwin. They see images of mainly blond, sun-tanned people with white stuff on their lips, cavorting around in baggy shorts in a variety of board-based water sports, or toasting wild mushrooms around campfires, and they think this lifestyle will somehow suit them and they'll be really good at it. But they won't and it won't. It'll be horribly hot, wet and full of people who say 'awesome' a lot and have Facebook pages full of photos of themselves and an unfeasibly large gang of mates, gurning into the camera. Baden-Powell could surely never have envisaged this nightmare scenario.

Tying Knots

Forget the moral codes and principles of honesty, decency and fair play. The greatest legacy of the Scouts is tying knots. Why, cry the traditionalists, can no one tie a decent knot any more? I'd rather ask – apart from tying your shoelaces, when has it ever been of any use to be able to tie a knot? I don't recall ever having been late for work because the bowline on my Boatswain's Chair wasn't tied properly, or my flock of lambs escaping on to a motorway because my sheep-shank was faulty. Knot-nutters claim that the uses of knots are endless, like when you are trying to reduce the amount of sail you have in a strong wind or tether your horse to a post. As only a lunatic would get into a sailing boat in a strong wind or go near a horse ever, never mind to sit on it, I think we can give knots a miss. My attitude to knots is summed up by Alexander the Great, who was faced with the mind-boggling complexity of the Gordian knot, which had defeated everyone who had tried to unravel it. So he took out his sword and chopped it in two. The truth is, there are so many different types of knot only because sailors were so bored on their year-long voyages that they whiled away the hours by inventing pointless agglomerations of string. It was either that or fiddle with themselves for months at a stretch (after which, it probably would). It isn't the case that all knots are useless; here are the few knots that are worth 'knowing' how to tie, or untie.

Balloon knot (keeps kids happy)

PlayStation controller knot (keeps teenagers happy)

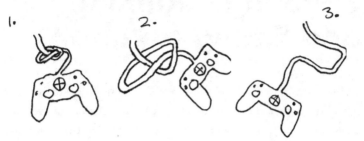

Bin-bag knot (keeps wives happy)

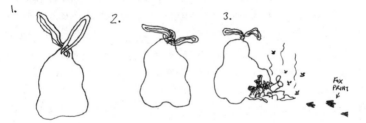

Alan Knott (keeps wicket)

Shooting, Skinning and Eating a Rabbit

In these straitened times food is growing scarcer by the day and pretty soon we will have to hunt, shoot, cook and eat all our own food. Oh, hang on a minute, no we won't. Despite the worst financial collapse ever in history since the last one, despite global food shortages and rocketing fuel costs, we still seem to have about three supermarkets in every town, all of them packed to the gunnels with food and people trying to buy it. There is so much meat in these supermarkets that they don't even have to stock rabbit. Who wants to eat that anyway? I can't even look at a skinned rabbit since I saw Roman Polanski's film *Repulsion* (check it out, or, on second thoughts, don't). Why on earth, then, would you want to go off into the fields with an air rifle and try to pop Peter Rabbit in the eye with an airgun pellet, unless you were some kind of sadist. The very idea of encouraging young people to even think about taking pot-shots at living things is crazy. Why not go the whole hog and print the instructions for making your own dirty bomb?

Many authors and columnists who have climbed on to the 'back to the old ways' bandwagon, have put forward the notion that we are somehow obliged to find out how the meat we eat gets on our plate and get some appreciation of the work involved. One of these is Hugh Fearnley-Whittingstall: fortunately for everyone, Hugh not only bangs on about the need to know where our food comes from, he shows us by rearing and slaughtering animals in his lucrative TV shows and books. So thanks for that, Hugh, that means I don't have to do it and I get to eat your excellent sausages too.

It's not just Hugh, though: there are many books that encourage you to immerse yourself in the guts of nature as if living like Robinson Crusoe was the only way to experience life properly. Not content with encouraging you to slot various wild animals, the Nostalgia Police suggest you should also take the skin of your dead rabbit and tan it. Why? From a practical point of view the skin of one rabbit would probably give you the leather for half a glove. From all other points of view it's a pretty revolting business. I think all the tanners in history would rise up from the grave and cry out with anger if they knew that people in the twenty-first century were being encouraged to muck around with tanning as if it was some kind of therapy. This is how *The Dangerous Book for Boys* describes it:

Various chemicals are used in the process including traditional ones derived from boiled brains or excrement... No one said it would be easy.

Alright, I won't bother then.

Identifying Trees

This is an essential part of what the Scout Movement call woodcraft, and who could fault it, really? Knowing the names of the things that surround you is important, and worth passing on to younger generations. But the sad thing about knowing the names of trees is that pretty soon it will be fairly useless. As a child I remember the classroom wallchart that had simple outlines of each tree, its leaf and its name. Unfortunately there is so much disease and pollution in most big towns, the same graphic could be used for the elm, the horse chestnut, the lime and the sycamore.

Probably more useful would be an illustration of the stuff that gets stuck in trees:

Tesco bag
Shoes
Kite
Tyre on rope
Remote-controlled plane
Suicidal teenager

Cadet Corps

There are plenty of people who are well up for all that the Scouting life can throw at them, but wish there was a bit more genuine excitement, by which they mean firing guns. The uniforms and the tent-based manoeuvres and the tracking people and animals through woods and tying them up with special knots is all very well, but couldn't there be some element of jeopardy? Some real explosions, armoured vehicles, lots of shouting and that sort of thing? Well, yes there can if you are lucky enough to go to a school where there's a Cadet Corps. Our present government (whoever that might be – at the time of writing Gordon Brown is up shit creek without a paddle or a canoe) is keen on encouraging Cadet Corps in all sorts of schools, because they argue that military discipline is good for young people, whatever their background. Yes and what could possibly go wrong in a school where teenagers are given access to weaponry? Some of it is even better than the stuff they use at home. Actually we don't have to speculate – we have the excellent British film *If*. If you haven't seen *If*, it was made in 1968 by the subversive director Lindsay Anderson and climaxes with a couple of renegade public schoolboys massacring the whole school on Founder's Day. Now although this is a common occurrence in most American schools, it might cause a few ripples in the UK if teenagers were to start rampaging through the science block with M16s. Unfortunately it looks like more of them will get the chance to put on another uniform over the one they're already wearing and take their place in a trainee death squad. I suppose in big cities like London and Manchester we won't really notice the difference and it all depends whether you prefer the person who beats you up on the way to the off-licence to have short hair and shiny boots.

Chapter Four
Proper Holidays

Foreign holidays are not what they're cracked up to be – I don't need to elaborate further on that theme (see *Can't Be Arsed*, still excellent value at £9.99) so, yes, a traditional holiday in England is actually right up my street.

But the British holidays of my childhood never quite match up to the authentic *Famous Five*-style adventure that the competitive holidaymakers and travel writers in the Sunday supplements boast about. This is what's known as a Boden Holiday...

· ·
Boden Holidays
· ·

What is Boden? If you have never seen the Boden posh mail-order clothing catalogue it's probably because they don't want you to see it. No one ever asks for a Boden catalogue – it somehow materialises on their doormat. Some sinister computer somewhere in Boden's cool, limewashed offices must have a postcode monitor and when it senses that a particular postcode has suddenly reached the required status, a red light goes on, something buzzes, an email is sent to someone who presses another button and about forty Boden catalogues magically appear in the postman's trolley – lo and behold, one fine Tuesday morning you are looking at a posh MILF in floaty knitwear sitting on some driftwood.

There also pages of young blokes, who look like they work in the City but are actually actors called Raiph, wearing stripey shirts and loafing around on pebble beaches with a dog or a cricket bat. The kids are always unfeasibly cool nine-year olds called Jake with blond mops who have already published volumes of poetry. As if this wasn't annoying enough when you look at the photographs closely you will see the small print. Somewhere on the page next to each model is their name and some kind of epigram giving you a glimpse of their 'personality', for example, 'India loves: *flying kites and the plays of Ibsen*', 'Zane is never happier than: *when I'm crazy*'.

It's a mystery to me how Boden receive any mail orders at all, given that so many people must rip the catalogue to shreds in a frenzy of hate.

Anyway, so that's Boden and a Boden holiday is pretty much

what is depicted in the catalogue – an improbably deserted beach in true *Famous Five* style, somewhere like Suffolk or Brittany; lots of driftwood, an old-fashioned beach-hut and utterly contented-looking adults floating around their carefree, confident children who clearly receive quite enough stimulation thank you from just throwing a pebble.

Although it may seem to be a fairly inexpensive way to spend a week or two of your summer holidays, the genuine Boden Holiday will somehow cost thousands of pounds and will be impossible for anyone else to re-create, and yet we are meant to believe it is the most natural thing in the world to do, and will put you back in touch with more innocent times when everyone went off on a horse and cart to go hop-picking.

But the worst aspect of the Boden Holiday is the bragging people do on return. It's a different kind of bragging from the traditional my-holiday-was-so-expensive-and-or-exotic-you-couldn't-begin-to-imagine-how-good-stroke-expensive-it-was kind of bragging. I can put up with that because I know, wherever it was, it would have been too hot, too dangerous and taken too long to get there for me. No, the really annoying thing about Boden Holiday bragging is you just know not a grain of it is true.

'*Oh, it was marvellous. Zak and Daisy just went off for hours pond-dipping and beachcombing, and we had a wonderful bonfire on the beach and barbecued some sea bass with samphire, it was idyllic.*'

Well, I'm sorry, love – hour after hour on an English beach, particularly the pebbled variety, can be mind-numbingly dull, as can any kind of beach holiday. If it's sunny you lie down and get hot; if it's windy you spend your whole day pinning down the corners of flapping blanket material, contorting yourself like a Twister champ. And if it's raining you sit in the car with the windows steaming up with your dad occasionally leaning back and clouting you because he can't hear the radio. My dad was an expert at back-seat clouting. He could usually cuff me and my two brothers with one swipe while smoking a Panatella and doing sixty on the Fosse Way.

The Slot Machine Embargo

Admirable though my dad's clouting technique was and despite the fun we had trying to wind him up, what really made our family seaside holidays were slot machines.

When you talk about slot machines now most people have the image of white-haired old ladies in shell-suits dropping thousands of dollars in the air-conditioned, perma-daylight hellholes of Las Vegas, or a seedy shop front in the seedy part of a seedy town with a sign saying 'over 18s only'. But for me slot machines were a children's paradise – the idea that anyone over the age of eighteen would want to go anywhere near them would have shocked me.

As soon as dad's car hit the seafront car park, and before the wind-breaker was erected, my brothers and I would be looking for the slots. Forget fishing in rock-pools, sandcastles, beach cricket and barbecuing samphire; give me the Penny Falls, the Teddy Picker, the sinister Jolly Jack Tar and the 2p horse-racing thingy any day. That so much metal and wood and plastic could be mobilised by electricity just to entertain me! It sent waves of giddy excitement up my spine.

I don't know how old a slot machine has to be before it becomes acceptable to Proper Game nostalgists, but for a kid, the more sophisticated and modern the better. When they introduced the first screen-based racing car game I was mesmerised, even though the steering wheel was attached to a celluloid car on a stick. And Pong, Space Invaders and Galaxian just made the whole experience even better. The atmosphere of spun sugar, cigarette smoke and deep fat frying are as redolent of the seaside for me as a gust of salty air.

But for the Proper Childhood Police none of this will do. Slot Machines are somehow not authentic enough and there is a limited range of activities allowed on to the programme for a 'Proper' Holiday.

Beach holidays approved by the traditionalists must involve rock pools, nets, beach cricket, flying a kite, making sandcastles, burying family members in sand, paddling, skimming stones. Here are the reasons for not bothering with any of them.

Skimming Stones

In all those books about *What Every Dad Should Know* (you should know the ones I mean by now) you will find an entry on Skimming Stones. As every dad is required to know how to do this, it's doubly embarrassing when you can't. The truth is that the game is stacked heavily against you. Apparently, the optimum angle of the surface of the stone to the water is 20 degrees and you'll be damned if you've brought your protractor on holiday with you. One stone in five hundred is vaguely flat enough and even then you'll be lucky to get any more than four bounces – the world record is 51 by the way. The more pathetic your results, the more angry and reckless you become, putting more and more unfocused effort into each throw.

So, if you're by the seaside, you may end up braining a careless swimmer on the first bounce, and if you're really wound up, a surfer. To lighten the mood, give yourself 10p for every time you hear someone say, 'That's the principle Barnes Wallis used to develop the Bouncing Bomb'.

Kite Flying

The Chinese, of course, claim to have invented kites, just like they are supposed to have invented everything else. Frankly, I'm fed up of hearing that everything from gunpowder to forks to coffins to Radio 4 was invented in China.

However, let's give them kites – they were certainly the first to send people up in them to spy on enemy soldiers and throw stuff at them. Strangely, it never occurred to them to drop bombs made with their bloody gunpowder. Maybe they were too busy inventing the sausage and the cricket bat?

What the Chinese didn't realise is that kites could be lethal weapons in themselves. The Kite-flying Code – yes, there really is such a thing – is about twenty pages long, so numerous are the ways of killing people or yourself with one kite. Benjamin Franklin almost became the first person to die while pissing about with a kite when he deliberately flew it into a storm cloud to see if he could tempt the lightning out. Science has come a long way since then, of course, and the power of electricity has been harnessed, to be zapped across the country on overhead powerlines, which are suspended at the perfect height to catch new generations of kite-flyers and fry them to a crisp, just as the circle of life intended.

The other ways you can kill or maim with a kite is by hitting an aeroplane (yes it does happen), landing it on a dog, crashing it onto a child's head, allowing the string to slice through your fingers like cheese wire or sprinting along the edge of a cliff top, looking backwards at the kite as you drag it behind you and plummeting over the cliff's edge like Wile E Coyote.

Glamping

The early years of the twenty-first century has seen the invention of some truly appalling words – skillset, heads-up, wannabe, upskill, abs, core, apps, twitter, deliverables argh argh argh argh aaaaaaarrrrggghhh! But one of the worst, the very, very worst, is 'glamping'. It's constructed from the word 'glamour' shortened to 'glam' which unless it refers to 'glam-rock' is one of the most hateful abbreviations ever – up there with 'goss', 'Li-Lo' and 'luxe' – and added to the word 'camping' – still one of the most pointless activities ever.

Glamping seems to have originated, although I can't be sure of this, in the requirements of part-time hippy twats who insist on going to music festivals like Glastonbury or worse still, Latitude, and want to hang on to their middle-class comforts. So what you get when you go glamping is a choice of bell-tents, teepees, yurts and eco-pods that are pitched on grass but are equipped with iPod docks and compost toilets. Like staying at home essentially, but, you know, more people.

Another variation on the glamping theme is the caravan – but because the average glamper thinks they are far too hip for the formica and shag-pile explosion that is to be found in most modern caravans, they disport themselves in Airstream trailers – highly polished American bullet-shaped caravans manufactured around the time of the Great Depression. But because these Airstreams are now owned by the Boden/Innocent Smoothie type of 'green' entrepreneur, they are considered cool and somehow ethical.

You will find in the pages of many a clothing-and-pointlessly-expensive-knick-knacks catalogue (not just Boden) dreamy hippy-chicks in flowery dresses hanging out of Airstream trailers, holding hands with their beautiful nine-year-old daughters with braided hair and unsettling amounts of make-up. As soon as the photo shoot's over they'll be off with their butterfly net or playing outdoor chess with pieces made from locally sourced renewable timber.

Again these glamping holidays are just another form of boasting for those people who like to impress the rest of us with their overt longing for the simple life, their desire to save the planet, their eagerness to stand apart from the crowd and their effortless ability to enjoy themselves wherever they are.

Playing with Dogs

Ah! A boy and his dog –the classic combination. Shaggy and Scooby, Tintin and Snowy, Belle and Sebastian; the slobbering, snuffling, bum-sniffing canine has been the traditional sidekick for any chap on an adventure, particularly on holiday. Even boys who are actually girls like George from the *Famous Five* had Timmy the Dog to discover secret passages on Kirrin Island and see off ruffians and criminal-types.

But however brilliant dogs may be – and I do like a good dog – what do they do on holiday except bark at the sea and chase unfamiliar wildlife? Oh yes, and they leave turds on the beach, and shake sand in your tea and come running up to you with their salivary tennis ball and drop it into your chips. And make you stay in rubbish accommodation because no one wants a dog messing up their hotel.

That's the problem with dogs: you're lumbered with something that not everybody likes and they're a huge commitment and a responsibility; not just because they demand as much of your time as kids do, but because you have to teach them all the basic stuff like who not to bite, which leg not to hump, when it's appropriate to lick the testicles and where not to poop. This might seem a pretty obvious thing to say, although to look at the way some people handle their dogs where I live, you'd think none of it had ever occurred to them. And for every person who can't control their dog, there's another who *won't*. Let's not forget that, as well as Shaggy and Scooby, we have Hades and Cerberus, Bill Sykes and Bullseye, Sid and Scud from *Toy Story*.

And this brings us to the other general problem with dogs, particularly with regard to your personal safety: what happens when they meet another dog? Bum-sniffing if you're lucky, but my early teenage years out walking with my dog are crowded with images of vicious scraps and the occasional bite-mark from trying to separate a couple of snarling beasts. And then the dogs would start fighting. This was in a bleak South Yorkshire mining village – it's even bleaker now the industry has all gone and yet the less suitable an area is for a dog to live, the more dogs there seem to be, and huge-headed massive-jawed devil-dogs they are too.

Dog wounds cost more to fix now than human ones. So when some pin-headed idiot's pit bull makes a bee-line for your mutt, you're probably going to be better off picking your own dog up and letting the attack dog sink its fangs into *you*. Or you could employ the most useful dog-trick ever, and grab the attack dog's front legs and yank them apart. You'll then have to deal with the irate owner of the late-lamented pet, but you might have saved yourself some hefty vet's bills.

Swimming in Ponds and Rivers

Who wants to swim in a swimming pool? Surely a river or a stream or a lake is a much more natural place?

Well actually I'd rather not swim in either. Getting into any water more than a foot deep is asking for trouble, unless you're at home having a bath. Lord knows public swimming pools are

revolting enough but at least they're only mildly dangerous and smelly. Outdoor swimming is in a different stinky death-trap league altogether.

But would you believe there's now a growing and deeply disturbing movement for a return to 'natural' swimming? It's trying to evoke the spirit of Huckleberry Finn and Tom Sawyer; of stripping off and diving naked into the creek or the old swimmin' hole. This was in the 'Weekend' section of a broadsheet newspaper recently:

Outdoor swimming gives you a craving for a simpler, more honest way of life... It is cousin to organic food, nephew to slow living and brother to our collective yearning for the wild ...

It's also the perverted uncle of submerged bedsprings and the wicked stepmother of ankle-grabbing weeds, aggressive pikes, dangerous currents, discarded fish-hooks, hidden shallows to break your neck on, hidden depths to suck you under, broken glass, used syringes, turds, weirs and Weil's disease from the gallons and gallons of rat urine that the buck-toothed bastards pump out on a daily basis.

'No, no, no!' say the skinny-dippers. We have been frightened away from our natural habitats by the scaremongers, they say. We were born to mess about in rivers and we shouldn't be deterred by the nanny-state. Here's that 'Weekend' journalist again:

The clear water is soft and limpid. I have a flashback to childhood; I flip onto my back and The Wind in the Willows *floats into my memory.*

In *The Wind in the Willows*, you'll remember, they always used a boat mainly because Ratty kept pissing in the water.

Pond-dipping

This is supposed to be hours of fun. In fact if you were to believe some people, this is all their kids do on holiday for a whole week. You need a net on a stick for pond-dipping – no one ever brings one on holiday with them, but the local beach shop will happily sell you one (because they saw you coming) for about ten quid.

Then you wait for the tide to go out and see where the rock has caught the sea in little nooks and crevices. Clamber over the slippery, green and slightly smelly rocks and fall over, bashing your elbow or grazing your ankle. Climb up again and find a suitable rock pool. Take a good look; concentrate on the water's edge or the delicate fronds of seaweed; you may need to shield your eyes from the reflections on the water. Go on; look closely – what can you see? Nothing. Nothing at all. Some seaweed and pebbles and green gunk. There is never anything in rock pools except rock and pool. The clue is in the name, d'you see? In all the hours I have spent looking in rock pools (OK, seconds, then) I have never seen so much as a winkle. I have looked on-line at a website called 'virtual rock-pool' and it tells me I could see tiny porcelain crabs, microscopic fish called blennies and even a hydra. It also shows you diagrams of what these amazing creatures look like and honestly, you'd have as much fun looking for woodlice under your carpet.

Burying Relatives in Sand

As I child I have very vivid holiday memories of my brothers burying me in my little inflatable canoe on the beach at Cleethorpes. Yes, I can clearly remember how much I hated it. It was occasionally no fun for my brothers either as all children's spades in those days were made of metal and there's nothing more painful than a spade blade slicing through the sand into your little toe. And you should be careful it doesn't become 'entombing relatives in sand'. In one recent year in the United

States over fifty people were killed or injured digging holes that were too deep or unstable. I have seen man-made holes in some beaches that were so deep you'd expect to find Arne Saknussemm down there.

The holes that don't collapse often serve as highly effective man-traps for anyone taking a walk on a beach at dusk. Whatever amusement you might get from seeing an unsuspecting stroller suddenly disappear down your sand hole would be tempered by the £30,000 law-suit that accident-lawyers are now slapping on careless beach-diggers.

Look, I know it's boring but why don't you just sit on the beach and sunbathe?

Waterboarding

This is a slightly misleading title. I'm not talking about the CIA-approved method of torturing Al Quaida suspects. I mean anything to do with people putting flat pieces of wood or plastic on water and perching on top of them. There are loads of them and each new one you learn about turns out to be more stupid than the previous one.

Here's a list, and I haven't made any of them up:

Surfing – the father of all other board watersports; borderline acceptable if only because of the Beach Boys and Dick Dale.

Flowboarding – Surfing on an artificial wave machine. You stay where you are and the water is fired at you. Why would you do this? It's like sitting on a mechanical bucking bronco and pretending you're a cowboy.

Skurfing – exactly like water-skiing but on a surfboard. Risible.

Wakeboarding – like waterskiing but with one board attached to both feet. So exactly the same as Skurfing.

Wakeskating – like wakeboarding but the board is not attached to the feet. Call it wankskating.

Kitesurfing – like surfing but you're attached to a kite. Or preferably a scud missile.

Parasailing – like kitesurfing except it's not a kite it's a parachute and you have no board. Or brain.

Skimboarding – you throw a tea-tray into shallow water and stand on it. 'Hey, dude, knock yourself out.' No, go on, really.

Bodyboarding – ah yes, the really annoying one. Whenever you go to a posh beach in a posh bit of England you'll find people in wetsuits, like they're in *Baywatch* or *Thunderball* or something, dragging a bit of polystyrene on a string. This is a bodyboard. Then they pull the polystyrene a few feet out into the water and lie down on it. It probably cost fifty quid to hire all the stuff (which takes about two hours to get ready) and another fifty quid for some bleach-blond wastrel to 'teach' them how to do it. They do this for about ten minutes and think that constitutes a good time.

Snow Holidays and Winter Sports

As far as I'm concerned any winter sport starts off at a slight advantage because it is always cold. Or so I'm led to believe; I've never actually been on a snow holiday – what a letdown it would be to travel all that way for the snow and then break out in a sweat?

Really though, I love snow – who doesn't? But there's a big difference between enjoying a snowball fight or building a snowman and careering down a mountainside with nothing to stop you except a tree trunk or someone's face. I can see how crossing terrain on skis or snow shoes is a necessity for an Inuit or a Laplander, but why all the Alistairs from Islington have to do it every year is beyond me.

A skiing holiday would be particularly dangerous for me as I don't think my blood pressure could cope with being stuck in a holiday resort with other people on a skiing holiday – the sort of people who, when they get home, have conversations with other people about whether they 'had good snow'. Also, no one seems to go on holiday to places where it snows a lot to do anything other than travel across it in one way or another, which is baffling – people don't go to the seaside and spend all their time traversing water and asking for trouble (some do though, see p128). Around February/March time the appearance of fracture-casts on the legs of the middle-class are as much a foretaste of spring as crocuses and snowdrops. Of course, no method of snow-based self-propulsion is safe, and yet there are plenty of them:

Snowboarding – Your feet are strapped to a single plank and you have to somersault over small hills. The catalogue of serious injuries to snowboarders would be tragic if they weren't all such annoying 'dudes'.

Luge – A suicidally tiny tea-tray upon which you lie face up and heave yourself down a hill.

Skeleton – A suicidally tiny tea-tray upon which you lie face down and heave yourself down a hill.

Bobsleigh – Several men hurtle down a steep slope in a tin bath. Either one of most dangerous sports you can imagine or the more hilarious alpine equivalent of *Last of the Summer Wine*.

Skiing and shooting – This is now a Winter Olympic event. You're out of breath after skiing across country and through a forest for a couple of miles. You pick up your rifle to aim at a target but your heart's beating and your hands are shaking and you accidentally shoot a friendly old woodcutter in the head. Call me crazy, but wouldn't it be more sensible to ski and shoot on seperate days?

Ice Skating – Much beloved of the people who promote 'frost fairs' and 'German Markets'. It seems nowhere in Britain can celebrate Christmas properly without a few log cabins selling Löwenbräu, frankfurters, gingerbread, and an ice-rink full of hestitant shoppers tottering around in a clockwise direction. Ice-skating has got to be one of the most over-rated and visually misleading pastimes ever devised. It all looks so relaxing, gentle and serene and yet the skating boots are cripplingly uncomfort-able, your ankle ligaments are stretched to snapping point and the ice is covered with an inch-deep film of slushy water, into which your children insist on dunking their backsides. Everyone is warned about the danger of falling over and having your fingers sliced off by a passing skater. However, if I ever allow myself to be dragged along to an ice rink again I'll deserve it.

Speed Skating – Imagine you are out strolling like the Duke of Edinburgh (with one hand behind your back), except you're dressed like a sperm and your thighs are the size of zeppelins.

Ice Blocking – To quote from Wikipedia, 'a recreational activity in which individuals race to the bottom of a hill sitting on large blocks of ice'. Hmm – what could possibly go wrong?

Wok Racing – Wikipedia describes Wok Racing as 'a sport developed by the German TV host and entertainer Stefan

Raab'. Basically, you sit in a wok and race it down an Olympic Bobsleigh run. Stefan is a German butcher turned TV presenter and musical comedy act. He once released a record called 'Wadde Hadde Dudde Da?' That should be warning enough.

'Dads and Lads' Holidays

Since the Proper Childhood Police appeared, thousands of dads have begun to feel guilty for not mucking around with their kids like those clean-cut square-jawed pipe-smoking gents from the knitting patterns.

But here's the truth – dads never actually did that sort of thing. Transport yourself back thirty or forty years (if you can) when the middle-aged people were growing up, and try to remember when your dad wasn't asleep most of the weekend after a long forty-hour week of manual labour (we used to make things and dig stuff out of the ground in those days, remember?).

My dad was a role model in all sorts of ways but he didn't play with us much. And we never had heart-to-heart conversations. The very idea of that would have had us all clenching our buttocks so tightly we could have cracked walnuts. Dads in the 50s and 60s told their kids what to think and how to behave; nobody was trying to 'bond' in those days.

Which makes the latest developments all the more peculiar. Because in the spirit of all the bollocks surrounding the *Dangerous Book for Boys* publishing 'phenomenon', fathers and sons all over the country are being thrown together on TV participation shows all about 'bonding'.

Todd Carty and his son help each other build a wigwam or Ian Botham and his son knock down a castle wall with a battering ram. It all reminds me of the brilliant cartoon series *King of the Hill* when Hank finally bonds with his lugubrious son by winning a 'Dads and Kids Doubles Shooting' event, narrowly beating the Bikini Chicks with Machine Guns.

Now the leisure industry has jumped on the bandwagon in style with 'Dads and Lads Holidays'. One website offering such a jaunt carries the slogan 'You love your son, now make him a friend'. Interesting use of the word 'make'.

Being a 'friend' with your dad is hardly a traditional, back to basics, pre-political correctness concept. Maybe when you pass the age of twattishness (25-ish) you can come to realise that your father was once like you (with less technology to amuse him), and you can start the long slow walk to friendship with him, which you might complete by the time you're 35 (giving you about five years before he dies on you). But I can guarantee that these were not notions any of us entertained as we turned ten in 1971. You either loved your dad because you admired him or he was funny or good at sports or you hated him because he spoilt your fun or, like a friend's dad once did, forced you to watch as he burned your collection of treasured comics.

There are some less than enticing prospects on the 'Dads and Lads' holiday, not least the other Dads and Lads. One of the things you do as a kid, looking up to your father, is rubbish the same things and people as he does, and Dads like nothing better than rubbishing other Dads' cars, houses, wives, trousers and general existence. So being stuck in a log cabin somewhere in the mountains with a load of other people to take the piss out of probably would result in a greater sense of camaraderie with your father but might also end in a fight.

Also, for some reason these 'bonding' holidays in the wilderness have electric light and running water but no television. As if you can share any meaningful quality time with your dad, or any other man for that matter, without a sofa and a television to be silent in front of together.

But, oh dear, there are board games (see page 43), a camp fire (see *Can't Be Arsed* – still excellent value at £9.99) and, get this: 'a singsong led by a Dads and Lads singer songwriter with acoustic guitar'. My heart sinks so deeply at the sound of these words, that I'm in danger of excreting it. I can only hope that the sounds of strumming and singing would be drowned out by the wincing and cringing of the audience.

Rites of Passage

There is a notion that rough and tumble adventure holidays, particularly with dad, or a male teacher, or a CRB-checked Scout Leader, or a radicalising imam are the best kind for a growing kid because they are harking back to the culturally rich rites of passage we all used to undergo in more primitive societies.

But this is the great thing about civilisation. We've moved on, and I think most people would be damn glad that we have progressed enough to remove the need for these rituals, if they knew how deeply unpleasant most of them were.

Some completely barmy groups think that even though we may be horrified to learn what various different tribes used to inflict on young people, we should be coming up with new rites of passage that mark a boy's arrival into manhood. They put stuff out on their websites saying things like:

> *Rites of passage are important in showing a boy when he should start thinking of himself as a man, when the community should start respecting him as a man, and when he should start shouldering the responsibilities of a man. Unfortunately, many young men today are never sure when they've really 'manned up'.*

Excuse me while I vomit. That's better. Yes, there is a bit of a problem with the blurring of the lines between adult and children in some aspects of modern life but why make such a big deal out of the moment of transition? As the surfing dude turtle in *Finding Nemo* says to Marlon who's asked him how he knows when his kids are ready to fend for themselves: 'When they know, you'll know, you know?' It's ironic that the notion of a rite of passage is championed so strongly by people who want their kids to be strong and independent and yet these rites represent parental interference of the grossest kind.

Take the **Mandan** – a tiny tribe of North American Indians.

According to the few people ever to have observed them, the boy who is about to be initiated has wooden splints hammered into his arms and legs. Then ropes are tied to the splints and he's hoisted above the ground while the skulls of his ancestors are placed on the ends of the splints (what did *they* do wrong?) and he's left there until he passes out with pain. Then – are you still with me? – he has his little finger chopped off as a sacrifice to the gods and finally the other villagers gather round him and yank the wooden splints out.

Not surprisingly, the Mandan are few in number. You can imagine how easy they were to overcome in battle. The enemy tribe spies them from a distance – '*Hey look at those nutters from the Mandan tribe. They are sticking bits of wood into themselves and chopping off each other's fingers. Let's wait until they're all disabled and we'll take over their whole village.*'

The Faroe Islands have a particularly gory ceremony to mark a boy's passage to manhood that involves them slaughtering dolphins. The dolphins are herded towards the shore and kids wade out with their dads and hack the dolphin to pieces with big knives. We must bear in mind that the Faroe Islanders are very weird people, living so close as they do to Norway and given that they hardly ever see daylight and that their national football team's goalie used to wear a bobble hat. It is also understandable, given the importance of the sea to the Faroes economy, that their sons' coming of age ceremony should be tied up with how they will be expected to make a living, but does it have to involve the really gruesome side of it? I work in television, but when my sons come of age I won't be forcing them to stand around at an awards ceremony making small talk with a load of wankers while totally undeserving tosspots walk off with all the prizes, will I?

Some **Aboriginal tribes** used to practise group circumcision. That's not everyone having their foreskin cut off at the same time. That's a group of older blokes gathering round a twelve-year-old, holding him down and slicing away with a piece of flint. It's OK though, because the kid has a stick to bite on for pain relief.

Worse is in store a few years later when the boy is about fifteen. He's surrounded by the elders again – you'd think he'd give them a wide berth by now – and this time they get a pointy stick and drive it through his urethra near the base of the old chap. This wound is never allowed to close up but to ensure that the various fluids don't splurt out whenever nature calls, the hole is plugged with a piece of wood.

Some anthropologists claim this as proof that the aborigines were the first people in the history of the world to develop a form of contraception, and for men at that. Well, as a contraceptive, an open wound in the knob with a piece of wood sticking out of it is going to be pretty effective for both parties.

Of course, not all Aboriginal rites of passage were so extreme. Other tribes when the time comes simply knock out a young man's incisor with a rock and throw it in the general direction of his mother's birthplace. Because, y'know, there's nothing like a bit of random specificity to pep up your mindless violence.

Vanuatu

The young bucks on this South Pacific island enter man's estate via the bungy jump. I've written extensively about this elsewhere *(Can't Be Arsed,* still excellent value at £9.99) and for a lot of young men from the West it has great appeal. These are, of course, very stupid young men.

Vanuatu-ans are actually a pretty extreme bunch and they use creepers for their death-defying leaps, not huge elastic strings. The elders of the tribe (I'm beginning to think the elders spend a lot of time making stuff up for a laugh) calculate the length of the creeper, which will be tied around the initiate's ankle, to be just long enough to allow the jumper's head to touch the ground, but short enough to stop it smashing like an egg in a Gordon Ramsay omelette.

If you ever get to see the original footage of this ritual, narrated by David Attenbrough when he was just too old to try it out himself, you will get a sense of the doom and foreboding surrounding it, a bit like the scene in the remake of *King Kong* when they're trying to summon up the beast, or the bit in *Finding Nemo* when Gil the Angel Fish tries to get Nemo to swim through the filter. The plus point for the initiate in this ritual is that he gets to spend the whole day before his big jump swearing and slagging off anyone he wants in the village, including his parents. This begs the question: How would Western kids cope with only doing that for one day?

Sparta

People who yearn for a proper upbringing for their children will often have a number of eras into which they wish they could parachute their offspring. The 1950s, with its back and sides as short as the trousers; the Victorian era where children had to make do with nuts for Christmas presents or, if they were really lucky, a hoop and stick. But when it comes to making children feel as brutalised and deprived as possible the original and best society was that of the Spartans of Ancient Greece – immortalised by the various camp movie renditions of the legend of *300*, according to which they ran everywhere, ate gravel and fought pitched battles in their pants.

The Spartans big idea was the *agoge*, which means 'taking

away'. The local government child-catcher would take 7 year-old boys from their mothers, herd them into a camp and subject them to a 22 year regime of rigorous training in armed combat, unarmed combat, deception, survivalist techniques, thievery and compulsory buggery.

It's a myth that all infants were routinely exposed on a hillside at birth to see if they were tough enough. What actually happened is they were first immersed in wine, then if they survived that they were brought before something a bit like the Jedi Council. If the council thought they looked a bit puny they were taken up a mountain and thrown down a chasm. These were the lucky ones.

The chosen ones, after about five years of being fed just enough to keep them alive (provided they learned how to steal enough food to supplement the porridge) were handed over to an older Spartan who would 'form a relationship' with them. It's not exactly clear whether this was a way of fostering ultra-platonic ties with an older mentor or simply a paedo's charter; either way the young lad had no choice in the matter.

By the end of his military training the (by now very sore-arsed) adult male would be ready to take his place in the Spartan killing machine. This machine was so efficient, Sparta was able to keep its majority slave population under control and exist as an independent city state for hundreds of years, with no city walls. Quite remarkable, but on the other hand, the Spartans produced virtually no literature and their only legacy is the concept of a lack of comfort and the word 'laconic', which comes from an ancient name for Sparta, ('Laconia') and means being terse, cold, lacking in emotion and a bit like Gordon Brown.

Unsurprisingly this system has been much admired and

copied by the English public school system of the nineteenth and twentieth centuries, although it's actually more like being put into 'care' in modern-day Britain.

British Rites of Passage

So in Britain today, have the ties of religion, family and community been more or less hacked away? And what meaningful ceremonies and rituals mark the transition from boy to man, girl to woman or anything to anything? And does it matter if the answer is 'none'?

Well, people are still baptised, married and buried, Barmitzva'd and Confirmed, but even with religious ceremonies, the ages at which these things happen are not set in stone any more. And, let's be honest, in Britain almost all the significant stages in a person's life are marked with ceremonies based on beer. Eighteenth birthdays, engagements, passing a driving test, twenty-first birthdays, finishing an exam, decorating a lounge, thirtieth birthdays, cooking sausages outside, leaving one office to work in another, fortieth birthdays, publishing a book about 101 things not to do before you die...

None of this is very impressive, is it? We are culturally impoverished in a major way. Vomiting birthday boys and cackling hen-do's in the centres of our market towns on a summer's evening are not much of a legacy to leave behind for future generations of archaeologists and anthropologists to discover. Imagine the press conference in the year 3000 as the academics unveil the amazing fossilized remains of a hen party in Aylesbury:

'You can see quite clearly that the fabric of the wide-brimmed hat has remained intact –this would have been worn by the bride to be, the Hen as it were – it still has sewn into the brim a ring of 25 condoms to indicate the number of sexual partners. And scattered around are at least a dozen bottles of Bacardi Breezer….'

But while we can be rightly ashamed of our booze-addled society, there is every likelihood that future generations will actually revere the 21st century Hen Party and mourn the disappearance of this 'Rite of Passage', just *because* it belongs to a different era. And there you have, in a nutshell, the problem we have today with nostalgia. Just because something is old and doesn't happen as often as it used to doesn't mean it is good or worth preserving. We don't have to expose our children on hillsides or perform circumcisions without anaesthetic or jump off cliffs with jungle creepers tied around our ankles, just because some other slightly crazy people, who are deemed to be a bit more 'authentic' than we are, used to do that; just as we don't have to go on a camping, glamping, pond-dipping, hop-picking, or peat-cutting holiday just because these were the only recreational opportunities open to our forbears. I'm just waiting for the two trends to combine in the next big adventure holiday experience – Head-shrinking, anyone?

Non Essential Kit for Boys:

Fish Hooks

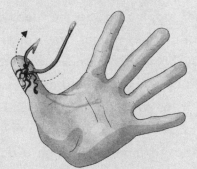

Believe it or not, fish hooks are deemed to be things no intrepid lad should be without – for fishing, presumably.

Yeah, go on, nip down to your local pond and catch a big one. And then what? Gut it and chop the head off, cook it and eat it? Let's see you do that, then … thought not.

Fishing is probably the most tedious, seedy, depressing way to waste eight hours of your life that I can possibly imagine. Apparently the enjoyment is in the solitude and contemplation as you wait for a fish to bite; the patience you learn as, like a Stylite or Buddhist monk, you challenge nature to mind games. And then the brief struggle as you reel the thrashing creature in and suffocate it in a bag or whack it on the head with a stick.

In theory, sitting on a teeming riverbank in springtime with the water lapping against the reeds as you eat watercress sandwiches sounds like a perfect way to spend the day. But in truth it's never a riverbank – it's more likely to be the skanky end of a reservoir or a gravel pit, or a canal in the arse-end of town, frequented by loons and perverts and copulating teenagers. And it's three o'clock on a dull winter's afternoon and all the other anglers are pissed or semi-suicidal or rummaging through their Morrison's bags for a porn mag. All in all not the best place for a happy-go-lucky lad in search of harmless fun to spend any time at all out of sight of his parents.

But back to the fish hooks. They're sharp and they pierce flesh easily; that's why they exist. So it should be no surprise when a person handling fish hooks on a regular basis impales a thumb on one. But never fear, help is at hand, as any decent angler's guide will tell you how to remove a fish hook from your person.

'You can easily remove a Fish Hook from the skin if the barb of the hook point is not below the skin surface. Pull it out and you're done with it...'

Oh, that wasn't too bad.

'...The difficult one is when the Fish Hook penetrates your skin beyond the hook barb. This procedure is excruciating.'

Ah. Well yes, it's got a barb on it so that it won't come out of Mr Trout's mouth easily. So I suppose it's not going to come out of your thumb without a struggle.

'First, push the Fish Hook in such a way that the hook point and barb come out in a different skin spot.'

Eeeeeaaaaaarrrrgggh. Yes, go on, push the hook further into your skin until the barb comes out somewhere else. Are you following this? And then what?

'With wire-cutting pliers cut the Fish Hook beneath the barb. Push back the Fish Hook out of your finger.'

Oh, damn it! If only you'd had wire-cutting pliers in your essential kit instead of that bastard pen-knife.

Chapter Five
Useful Knowledge

In the rush to take us all, fathers and sons together, back to basics, traditionalists and champions of 'the old ways' have not just drawn up a list of activities and games we should rediscover; approved knowledge is also now on the agenda. There was an appalling TV programme a few years ago called *That'll Teach 'Em* which aimed to show that modern teenagers were thick and couldn't cope with the rigours of a 1950s-style grammar school education. Children, it argued, learned nothing useful today and the basic stuff of History, Maths and Grammar were in danger of being lost forever because of the trendy-lefties who decide what our children should learn. So now there is a whole body of knowledge about battles and dates and Great Men; how to calculate the surface area of a cone and how to correctly use the semi-colon, which has become even more politically charged than it was before. All those new titles called *Stuff that Every Boy Should Know* should now have in parenthesis, 'and some schools won't teach them'.

• • • • • • • •

Latin

• •

Despite all the claims made for the benefits of a 'classical' education, if you were ever actually taught Latin at school, you will know that it's only good for showing off. Children who swan off to Latin while their mates are doing physics or domestic science or technical drawing are effectively wearing a badge proclaiming their superior brain power and correct use of the subjunctive. They also have a sticker on the back of their blazer saying 'please kick me and flick my ears whenever you feel like it'.

Latin may open the door to great literature and history but only if you can be bothered to read Penguin translations of Virgil and Horace and Tacitus or watch *I, Claudius* on television. No one's going to bother deciphering twelve books of the Aeneid or the Annals of Tacitus from the original Latin for fun. I for one never really got the hang of Latin and after a double period of Livy on a Friday afternoon, I certainly wasn't going to spend my weekend looking for the verb in one of Cicero's sentences.

Latin's only use to me – apart from showing off – was to get me into Greek, which, in the end, got me into university. Greek is a far superior language – it has more words, easier sentence structure and allows people to say to you, 'It's all Greek to me!' which only becomes annoying after the fiftieth time.

Greek is certainly not going to help you avoid the accusation of showing off but because so few people know that it is actually a toff's subject you will not get into much trouble. Greek is a kind of Stephen Hawking subject – you are assumed to be a kind of weirdo or an extreme boffin, verging on the handicapped. Latin is commonly known as an overtly arrogant discipline that makes you look like a twat – more Dawkins than Hawking.

The Greeks were never ones for boasting. The Romans, on the other hand, were always at it. Cicero is held to be one of the worst culprits ('Oh, happy Rome, born when I was Consul!') perhaps only because so much of his work survives, but the whole of Roman society was set up for overly ambitious bigheads. They invented the idea of 'a career', the *cursus honorum,* which established official jobs which people could only attain at certain ages. Of course anyone who held an office at the youngest possible age (*in suo anno*) was considered to be going places, but if you hadn't made Praetor by the age of forty, then forget it, loser. *Curriculum vitae* is not a Roman invention but did you ever see anybody write it in Greek?

Weirdly, having invented a system that encouraged it, the Romans tended to combat ambition and arrogance with death. The Athenians had a much better way of dealing with things – ostracism. Anyone in Athens who was felt to be getting a little above themselves was simply banished to another country. The people would write their name on a broken piece of pottery (an *ostrakon*) and the person with the most votes got the heave-ho. It's a revealing measure of British civilisation that 2,500 years later we have developed sufficiently to use the same system for TV game shows.

Of course, the worst thing about Latin, which Greek students never fall prey to, is the use of Latin phrases in normal conversation. *Primus inter pares, quae cum ita sint, mutatis mutandis, sine qua non, ad hominem, a priori* – none of these phrases are of any more use than the English equivalent. 'All things being equal' – what's wrong with that? 'First among equals' – pretty straight-forward, so why make a tit of yourself saying it in Latin?

Useful Knowledge

Peculiar *Daily Telegraph* columnists try to make money out of books which purport to show the validity of Latin as a modern language. Apparently it helps you with spelling and understanding what a doctor has written about you on his notes or what Monty Don is going on about in *Gardeners' World*. You can make *Carry On* jokes about Bilious and Querulous and say things like '*Caesar adsum iam forte, Quintus aderat*'. Brilliant! How have you coped without it all these years?

The best thing is to studiously avoid all use of Latin and when someone drops a Latin phrase into conversation, don't feel inadequate, don't play their game and scurry to a computer to look it up; just say – what does that mean?

LATIN CONJUGATIONS AND DECLENSIONS

Latin is supposed to be very useful for improving your English and Latin bores will tell you that of the words we use today have their origins in Latin. Here are some you may recognise and others which may not be so familiar.

Regular verb	(many Latin verbs end in the same way e.g.)	or also	
Amo	-o	-to	- bo
Amas	-as	-tis	- bis
Amat	-at	-tit (snigger!)	- bit
Ameobi	-amus	-timus	- bimus
Amadeus	-atis	-titis (fnaar!)	- bitis
Adamant	-ant	-titmus	- bint
	-dec	-tint	- bitch

The Romans were keen on sports of all kinds and may even have played the first form of football called 'Calcis', from the verb 'Calcio' meaning 'To calculate astronomically high wages'.

ronaldo	fabrego
ronaldis	fabregas
ronaldive	fabregat
ronaldamus	fabregamus
ronaldatis	fabregatis
ronaldunt (ancient rhyming slang)	fabricate (excuse for spitting)

Some obscure Latin nouns are still in use today:

video	rex	nemo
vides	regis	nullius
videt	regem	neminis
dvd	rege	neminem
blu-ray	ska	jay-z
sky+	bluebeat	p.diddy

Maths

No subject sums up the great divide between traditionalists and modernisers like Maths. Proper sums were ones that you did in your head or with a pencil and paper and included stuff like long division, long multiplication, the square on the hypotenuse, the surface area of a cone and if Jack has four apples and Mary runs a bath of water for three hours, how tall is Alan's dad?

Modernisers do weird things like number lines, vectors, sets and matrices. Maybe that's the sort of stuff that people who make computers and clever machines use these days. Maybe working out the surface area of a cone is no use to NASA, although most space ships do seem to have cones at the end. What I do know is that modern maths is a different language to the one I learned. This does not make me want to go crusading into my local primary school like one of the Knights Templar and slaughtering anyone who won't swear allegiance to The Slide Rule.

The invention of the calculator was one of the most wonderful things ever to happen to school children, and not just because, with clever use of numbers, you could write BOOBS, SHIT or LEEDS. By the time I took my maths 'O' level, calculators had advanced just about enough to able to fit inside an average-sized satchel, so although we were allowed to use them in the exam (the first time ever!), many of us couldn't even lift one so we didn't bother. But I don't begrudge young people their far superior technology – the calculator function on a mobile phone is probably the least interesting thing it can do. I think children should be allowed to Google the answers in exams, especially in maths and science; after all, isn't it perverse for science subjects to prohibit the use of one of science's greatest inventions?

Not surprisingly, many grown-ups don't share my view on this subject. Many parents feel that their children need to go right back to basics and fill their heads with so many number-combinations and rules and formulae that they become human calculators. It seems it's not enough for them just to know their times tables, which I didn't see the point of learning until I saw a brilliant computer game called Times Attack, in which you destroy monsters by working out the sums written on their scaly bodies. No, in addition to the times tables, young people are now, on a weekly basis throughout this country and all over the world, being herded into sheds and forced to learn *addition* by heart. That's stuff like $17 + 25$, $18 + 26$, $19 + 27$ and so on. This is called Kumon. It's Japanese, but don't read anything from that into the 'being herded into sheds' stuff. I'll be honest and say that I have never heard or read a bad thing about Kumon so this is all my own opinion but it seems to me *fucking ridiculous* to try and get kids to memorise addition combinations. How does that help you understand maths? My chemistry teacher once said to me as I asked yet another question about molar density: 'Don't understand it, just absorb it.' That pretty much put the tin hat on it for me and chemistry. The argument in favour of the Kumon method is that it helps kids do much better in tests than those who don't use it. And that basically is what it's all about; what this whole section is all about. Knowledge is for many people, particularly parents, a weapon with which you destroy the opposition.

Useful Knowledge

So good luck to all those who succeed in their maths exams and their plans for world domination, but heed this warning – being *too* good at maths is a really bad thing.

First, it means you will have at some point listened to a teacher explaining differential calculus and thought 'sounds interesting, I must find out more'.

Second, you are therefore bound to end up being a weirdo. Just look at any documentary about statistics, predictions, chaos theory or quantum physics (I hope you've got BBC4) and watch out for the creepiest, hairiest cross between a Hell's Angel and an accountant. Within seconds a caption will appear underneath him which reads 'Mathematician'. You've seen *A Beautiful Mind*, right? – he's a maths genius. Oh yes, and he is also insane. He sees dead people, no wait, wrong film … he creates people as figments of his imagination just because he is too good at maths and his brain can't handle it. Hardly a good advert for taking Maths at 'A' level, is it?

Third, throughout all the time it has taken you to turn into this person, you will have had no friends, either because of personal hygiene, or because you will have been getting top marks in all your maths papers and no one likes a smartarse.

Finally, you will develop a bizarre and twisted understanding of the Universe, which people like you see only as a set of numbers and equations. You will have conversations with other maths nutters about the need to establish the existence of particles with silly, made-up names like the Higgs Boson, and then go off with billions of pounds of everyone's much-needed cash to build a stupid circle of pipe-work under the Swiss countryside which will never work properly and establish absolutely nothing. Then you will say, 'Ah, but that in itself is significant!'

Mathematicians are so keen not to be left out in the cold of Weirdo-land that they try to make normal people believe that they too can be good at maths, if only they know the short cuts. These are a bit like the 'cheats' for video games except in video-game terms maths is about as fun to play as Pong with small bats.

TEN TOP MATHS TRICKS, TECHNIQUES AND SHORTCUTS

1. When adding two large numbers together, always do the easy one first.

2. When subtracting a bigger number from a smaller number, multiply the big number by 9. By the time you have done that, the other problem won't seem so important any more.

3. When multiplying any number by 4 simply double it, then double it again. You can use the same method on a builder's estimate.

4. If you are ever asked to find x and y, say you don't have it because you stopped buying Coldplay albums after *A Rush of Blood to the Head*.

5. If four people go for a drink and spend £55, divide it into £13 each except for the person who had the wine.

6. A problem like 'John has four apples, Mary has twice as many as Peter who has two less than John' is called a 'simultaneous

equation', meaning you may as well stare out of the window at Jacqueline Tilley playing netball at the same time as you're trying to work it out.

7. If you are multiplying any two-digit number by 11, take the two digits of that number and separate them and put the sum of those two numbers into the gap between them, unless the sum of the two numbers is greater than nine in which case put the units of the sum of the two digits into the gap and add the tens from the sum of the two digits to the digit on the left. Simple.

8. When multiplying any number by 9, hold both hands up and if the number you are multiplying is 8, hold that finger down and count the number of fingers on one side for the first number and on the other side for the second number. Unfortunately you will need the fingers of the other hand to hold down the eighth finger properly so, er, look, just forget I mentioned it.

9. If you are struggling with Integration, try giving up maths and maybe people will like you better.

10. Here is a genuine mathematician's chat-up line, in case you ever manage to hold a woman in conversation for more than thirty seconds. It's a real killer so don't spray it around willy-nilly; use it wisely. Are you ready? Here it is:

'Hello, if you were Sine squared and I was Cosine squared, together, we'd be one.'

Good luck with that, although don't be surprised if she says: 'You lost me at "Hello".'

● ● ● ● ● ● ● ● ● ● ●
Drama
● ●

Drama – there's something wrong with the word itself, isn't there? It should act as a natural warning sign, but no; it seems that taking the lead in a school play seems to be positively encouraged, if not the very pinnacle of childhood achievement. If you have ever been on the receiving end of a Round Robin at Christmas, in which your distant friends recount their family triumphs, you will have noticed that playing Hamlet in the school production ranks even higher than the 15 A+ stars and grade 8 piano. And who could begrudge a young person their place in the spotlight?

Well, me, actually.

I don't doubt it's great for their confidence and proves to them that they can assert themselves in front of a live audience. But my problem with it, and drama in general, is the effect it has on others around them. The presence of just three people in a classroom who are keen on drama is enough to encourage the teacher (who probably does dance classes in her spare time) to rope the entire class into a production of some kind of leggings-and-leotards horror show. Pity the poor saps in the top juniors at my kids' primary school who, whether they like it or not, have *all* been press-ganged into the production of *High School Musical*. I would rather run around the playing field in my vest and pants until the end of Time.

Then think about what will become of the young thespian as they move through adolescence: if no one is able to give them a good shake and bring them to their senses, they could well end up 'studying' drama at school and become addicted to ridiculous and pretentious acting behaviour, such as 'walking through sticky mud', 'enclosing space' and 'being completely made of wood' (Arnold Schwarzenegger must have been particularly good at this).

As the 'showing-off' drug tightens its grip on their life, they may be lured into a drama society at college or, even worse, enroll at Drama School. Before you know it, they will be submitting themselves to Trust exercises. These are designed to encourage a group of drama students to feel comfortable with each other, but given that much of it involves people you don't know massaging your shoulders, what average properly uptight British person could possibly feel comfortable with that? I like to think most of us would react like Christopher Moltisanti in the brilliant *Sopranos* episode when, in the middle of an acting class, he is asked to express his feelings towards another student without using words, so he punches him in the face.

Obviously if you are not comfortable with Trust exercises, they will have achieved their purpose of filtering out the normal people, leaving the hardcore of fruitcakes to get on with 'raising their awareness of kinaesthetic boundaries'. Another way they do this is with Falling exercises. They stand around in a circle and take it in turns to collapse like a falling tree on top of each other, hoping someone will catch them. Most drama students will be doing this in the pub later after a few bottles of rioja, so why they need lessons in it is a bit of a mystery.

That so much of this sort of stuff is applied to corporate team bonding and office away-days gives you an idea of how much bollocks abounds in drama school. Educationalists, behavioural psychologists, motivational coaches and drama teachers love to talk about Tuckman's sequential stages of group development, i.e. what happens when a collection of people, like say a theatre company, get together to put on a play. The best-known stages are: Forming, Storming, Norming, Performing. Serious academic research has validated this analysis of group behaviour, although with a group of actors the stages are best described as Shagging Each Other's Boyfriends.

If our dedicated thespian becomes a professional actor, the silliness does not stop. No one, apparently, can even think about going on stage without doing some essential warm-up exercises:

The Yawn-Sigh: A combination of a loud yawn with a deep exhalation of breath as if one has heard some predictable but depressing news, like no one's coming to see the awful play you're in.

The Head Roll: Not, as you might think, the director's head when the play becomes the inevitable critical and financial disaster; but your own head should roll as if a string is attached to the top of your head and is pulling it off your shoulders. Ideally it should happen to all drama students.

The Face Stretch: Open your eyes and mouth as wide as possible expressing complete surprise, astonishment or horror, probably because that bitch Sebastian has stolen the scene again with his outrageous mugging.

Useful Knowledge

History and Historical Figures

We are supposed to use history to learn from humanity's most stupid and evil mistakes but most of the great figures we are meant to learn about in history – people who should inspire us and fire us to emulate their deeds – are, in fact, just dangerous nutters.

I would not advocate following the 'heroism' of **Admiral Lord Nelson**, for example. Yes, he was a brilliant tactician, brave, bold and delightfully insubordinate in his early career, but let's be honest, at the Battle of Trafalgar he was an irresponsible bigheaded idiot. Standing on the quarterdeck of the *Victory* in full view of everyone with all his medals and sashes achieved next to bugger all – he almost certainly got in the way of the various cabin-boys, boatswains and powder-monkeys trying to do a proper job. It was tantamount to sticking a target on his back and a big red arrow pointing to him saying, 'Lord Nelson, Admiral of the Fleet – why not have a pop?' Not only was Nelson killed at Trafalgar but several other people were cut to pieces by cannon fire as they followed him swanking about on deck. The fact is, genius though he was, Nelson got a lot of his own men

159

killed and all he had to show in return for it was the establishment of British naval supremacy for the next hundred years. I'd rather have my eye and my arm.

And what about **'The Charge of the Light Brigade'**?

Theirs not to reason why, theirs but to do and die?

What? Why was theirs not to reason why? Six hundred men on horses with swords and cardigans charging into cannons firing balls of iron five inches across? Why didn't any of them say – 'you're having a laugh aren't you?' Fifty years later people were still doing it but at least they were asking the question; at least the old lie – *'Dulce et decorum est pro patria mori'* – was being challenged. And I do apologise for the use of Latin there.

Let's not disparage the astonishing courage of those men but equally let's acknowledge the rank stupidity. And the fact that most officers were usually pissed when they rode into battle. (Many of the top brass at Waterloo were still hung over from the Duchess of Richmond's Brussell's Ball the night before.)

Chief among the officer idiots present at Sebastapol was **Captain Nolan**, the one who bungled the charge order. 'Attack the guns! Attack the guns!' he said. 'Bollocks will we attack the guns', should have been the reply. Not sure whether Tennyson could have made that scan.

Of course, Captain Nolan was carrying on the proud tradition of lunatic army officers; a tradition that survives to the present day with the likes of **Colonel H Jones**, who got the Victoria Cross at the Battle of Goose Green in the Falklands War for trying to head-butt an Argentine machine gunnest. We can marvel at the incredible bravery of soldiers in desperate situations but, remember, H Jones was a Colonel and his men were expected to follow him, crazy though he was.

So these characters are chiefly worth knowing about because they tell us what an extraordinary bunch humans are, but if you're looking for examples of behaviour to follow, I have my own list of dangerless role models. People who kept their heads down, avoided the limelight and generally got on with it.

Cautious Heroes for Sensible Boys

Quintus Fabius Maximus Cunctator Verrucosus

So Hannibal has slaughtered your best legions on your own soil and is rampaging throughout Italy, with his lethal cavalry and elephants, burning your towns and villages. You're the only big-shot Roman general left standing, so what do you do? Take Hannibal on in a great big all-or-nothing battle, trusting your luck to fate? No, you idiot, you are Quintus Fabius Maximus and you spend years actively avoiding confrontation. Basically you provoke the enemy then runawaaay!

A hotheaded political rival called Varro thought Fabius was a coward and said so in public. He led 90,000 Roman soldiers to the biggest defeat in Roman history at Cannae where 70,000 of them were killed. So much for boldness and 'bravery'. I'll bet Varro made his own bow and arrow when he was a kid.

Anyway, Hannibal got so frustrated with chasing Fabius around Italy and burning towns and villages that he decided, quite literally, to sod that for a game of soldiers. His men got tired and hungry – they'd rather stupidly set fire to all the crops to try and tempt Fabius to fight –and they all went back to Carthage in North Africa. That's a heck of a way to go, so they must have been pretty cheesed off. Hats off to Quintus Fabius Maximus for keeping out of trouble on an epic scale.

The Romans called him a cunctator – sounds pretty offensive doesn't it? But although it's not quite as rude as it sounds, 'The Delayer' was not exactly a flattering nickname. If you found yourself in a WWF-style wrestling bout (it could happen; I don't know what you're like) and you discovered your opponent was called 'The Delayer', you wouldn't exactly soil yourself, would you? In the end 'Cunctator' became Fabius Maximus' honorary title – part of his proper name (this would be a bit like Noel Edmonds' name being officially changed to Noel Bastard Edmonds), and Fabian tactics became recognised as a valid and valuable weapon.

David Batty

Most kids who want to be footballers want to be Wayne Rooney (without the chin, obviously) or Fernando Torres (without the girl's hair and face) or Steven Gerrard (without the beetling brow and hump). They see themselves curling in a free kick from 25 yards or dancing round the keeper and rolling the ball into the corner. No one wants to be the scruffy terrier-type who sits in front of the back four and dirties up the opposition strikers. No one wants to be David Batty, but they should.

The football pundits talk about Claude Makelele, once of Chelsea, as if he invented this role, completely forgetting that ten, fifteen years ago, every side had an unattractive ball-winning ruffian in midfield, and the best of these was Leeds United's David Batty.

Batty was the archetypal, unfussy, no-nonsense professional. He hustled and harried and pushed and shoved the opposition's fancy dans and did his best to stifle creativity. Then he'd give the ball to Gordon Strachan or Gary McAllister and with this midfield Leeds United won the last ever First Division championship, when football was a competitive sport and not, like it is now, a glorified form of banking.

As a role model for anyone who wants to avoid the limelight, David Batty puts Claude Makele in the shade. Consider this:

• Makelele's wife is the supermodel who wears M&S pants for a living. Batty's wife worked at Homebase.

• While at Chelsea, Makelele drove a Ferrari 360 and Mercedes McLaren SLR. While at Leeds, Batty drove a Ford Escort.

• Makelele is a multi-millionaire and lives in luxury in Paris. Batty has no credit card, he only ever uses cash and keeps the rest of his money in the Leeds and Holbeck Building Society.

• Makelele holidays in St Tropez, the Maldives and Cancun. Batty holidays in a static caravan. Probably.

Batty's won two league titles with different clubs and played 42 times for England and even refused to accept his Winner's Medal when he played for Blackburn as he'd missed so many games through injury he thought he didn't deserve it. We never hear him pronouncing on a defender's shortcomings on radio or television, or pretending to write a newspaper column – he's had his career and now he's spending his time with his family somewhere we don't know about.

David Batty, I salute you.

Cliff Thorburn

Two things stand in the way of Cliff's claim to greatness. 'Only two?' you say. Well OK, three, actually.

Number one – he's a snooker player.

Number two – his nickname was 'The Grinder'.

Number three – he's Canadian.

Now to be a Canadian snooker player with a particular reputation for being boring is a hell of a handicap to heroism, but I'm not picking out conventional heroes here. Cliff Thorburn is the living embodiment of Aesop's tortoise.

Cliff's greatest achievement was grinding down the most uncouth misspent youth ever to wear a waiscoat, Alex Higgins. Strutting around the table like Freddie Starr's Mick Jagger impersonation, Higgins would recklessly clatter reds and blacks all over the place, regularly clearing the table in less than five minutes. Higgins was the Hurricane, but in the World Snooker Championship final of 1980, he blew himself out on The Grinder. It was the triumph of sheer application over natural ability and a lesson to all the quiet, reserved and unexceptional people out there that said – 'just stick to what you're good at and let the flash bastards make the mistakes'.

Higgins went on to win other titles, the adoration of the public, the attention of the tabloids and, eventually, his place in the pantheon of wasted talents, alongside George Best, Gazza and Phil Cool. But only one more great achievement lay in store for Cliff – the first ever 147 maximum break in a World Championship. It won him fame and a sizeable fortune, almost as much as winning the tournament itself, but to be honest it was a bit too flashy for someone like Cliff Thorburn and he never won a major world-ranking tournament again. To be fair to Cliff, he continues to live a quiet and happy life with his family in quite a dull part of Canada, charging pretty reasonable consultation fees for anyone thinking of building a snooker room on the side of their house. What a blissful life!

St. Peter
It's fair to say that St Peter didn't actually avoid trouble. He went to Rome preaching Christianity at exactly the time that Nero was murdering Christians on a daily basis, and in the end he was crucified upside down.

What Peter famously did is disown Jesus when the chips were down. When Jesus was arrested, Peter could have said 'Take me as well', but he didn't. He almost crumbled under the interrogation of a servant-girl, who kept asking, 'Weren't you one of his disciples?' but he stuck to his 'must have been some other bloke' story until the cock crowed.

Now a lot of people might call that cowardice, but I'd call it pretty sensible behaviour, in the circumstances. Come on, there was no way Peter could have known for sure that Jesus was actually going to pull off the resurrection. At the crucial moment he thought – 'I'm not risking my neck for this. Curing lepers is one thing but rising from the dead?' So he ducked the issue, ran away and hid in a locked room with the other disciples.

Despite having let the side down, he didn't lose it completely and top himself like Judas. In the end he became the first pope, founded the Christian church and, having been put in charge of the keys to the Kingdom of Heaven, he received the honour of appearing in about fifty religious jokes.

Geoff Boycott

It's all very well for the likes of Viv Richards and Adam Gilchrist and Chris Gale and Flintoff and Pietersen to earn all the plaudits for bringing the carnival atmosphere to cricket with their big-hitting stroke-play, but Geoff Boycott made *prope*r runs. Nothing too flashy or risky; his job as the opening batsman was to see off the new ball and hold on to his wicket. Or, as Geoff would say, his wickeeet.

Geoff was a detail man and focused obsessively on his technique. Any little lad in the Headingley crowds, who had the courage to ask Geoff if they could bowl at him before the game might expect their puny deliveries to be slogged playfully over their heads for them to chase after. But that's a risky shot, is that, and you might get yourself out doing it. So Geoff would kill the delivery stone dead with his forward defensive until the boy got bored.

Geoff's relentlessly sensible technique and his devotion to his wicket meant he'd rather die than get out like David Gower, playing a shot like a girl, even if it meant he was still batting when it was dark and everyone had gone home.

Unfortunately this proved to be Geoff's undoing, both morally and professionally. People thought Geoff was more concerned about himself than the team, as evidenced by the number of batting partners Geoff seemed to run out. In the end, Geoff Boycott the personality became more important than Geoff the batsman and he wound up in court and the tabloids for knocking a woman about. Although I have to say Geoff's defence against the charge of assaulting his girlfriend was even more impressive than his defence at the crease: 'I work out twice a day. If I'd have hit 'er as many times as she said I did, 'er face would have been a bloody pulp.'

Sensible people don't end up in the tabloids, they keep their head down, their collar turned up, their elbow high, their front foot well forward and their bat straight. Geoff now makes his living telling people to do just that.

The Emperor Claudius

Anyone who has seen the *I, Claudius* TV series knows how Claudius the stammering, limping, twitching idiot became Emperor of Rome. And if you haven't seen *I, Claudius* shame on you, but here goes.

From Claudius's birth in 10 BC until he became Emperor in 41 AD three quarters of his family and about two-thirds of the nobility had been done away with by wars, poisonings, assassinations and judicial murder. He outlived one of history's great homicidal maniacs, Caligula (a first-century Joe Pesci only more violent and unpredictable), who terrorised and humiliated him on a daily basis.

But the really great thing about Claudius was that he didn't even want to become Emperor in the first place: he was a Republican and was almost forcibly proclaimed as Emperor by the Praetorian Guard who otherwise would have been out of a job after Caligula was assassinated.

Many historians think Claudius survived the horrors of post-Augustan Rome because he was considered an idiot and an embarrassment to the imperial family, with his drooling and stammering and twitching, and was pushed quietly into a cupboard where he could be forgotten about. But by the time he was in his late teens – ancient Rome's equivalent of middle age – people began to realise he was smart enough to make impressive speeches and write politically sensitive histories. So if his disability was a cover, he'd blown that quite early on.

Claudius was, clearly, a smart operator, with all the attributes required to qualify as a cautious hero. Patience, humility, endurance, an appreciation of when to keep your mouth shut; to laugh at other people's jokes and pretend to enjoy it when a lunatic gets you in a headlock.

Claudius, in fact, displays most of the hallmarks of **Plato's** ideal ruler – the **Philosopher King.** This is someone who doesn't want to be in charge at all but has to be forced to do it. Can you imagine Lord Nelson or Colonel H Jones being offered the chance of absolute power over Britain and saying, 'You know what? I think I'll leave it. Get Napoleon or someone to do it.'

Plato's point is that if the post of absolute monarch is open to people who *want* it, then there'll be competition which leads to ambition, aggression, violence and wars. The cultivation of a meritocracy with the biggest prizes going to those who try the hardest is in fact a recipe for disaster.

Andrew Ridgeley

How everyone laughed as George Michael dumped Wham! and headed off into the stratosphere, leaving the stupid-looking untalented one behind to fail dismally with his solo album and racing driver career!

But no one is laughing now, and furthermore I say we should salute Mr Ridgeley for one of the most dignified displays of former popstar behaviour since Bryan Ferry subdued a mental patient who was trying to crash the jumbo jet he was travelling on (Did you read that story? It was amazing).

Wham! were one of the silliest groups in the silliest period of pop music in the silliest decade ever. Not only were the early 80s ridiculous musically, they were ridiculous sartorially and tonsorially and Wham! excelled in all these categories. George Michael's hair was so big his face was in permanent shadow, making his orange skin all the more puzzling. His wardrobe, from teeny shorts to denim waistcoats to bafflingly bulky leather jackets, only served to distract you from the absurdity of lyrics like 'we've got plans to make, we've got things to buy and you're wasting time on some creepy guy'.

Where was Andrew in all this? Grinning and gurning and wobbling his head like a twat. And he may well have been playing the guitar on *Top of the Pops*, but it never sounded like there was a guitar on the actual records.

So many of the loons from the world of 80s pop have abandoned whatever self-respect they had left by taking to the road again. It seems like anyone who walked within a mile of a microphone or a synthesiser in those days is still scraping a living in front of audiences of students. Martin Fry, Carole Decker from T'Pau, Tony Hadley from Spandau Ballet, The Girl With The Big Hat from The Thompson Twins – they're all at it. The two gay Georges haven't had much success with preserving their dignity either, despite their huge stash of back-catalogue cash and critical acclaim.

But here's the lesson for us all to learn. For almost twenty years Andrew Ridgeley has done nothing. Nothing except marry one of Bananarama, move to Cornwall and get on with his life in a discreet, decidedly un-80s way. He doesn't do interviews, he doesn't dish dirt, he doesn't do comebacks. He's gone a bit grey at the sides and does a bit of shopping. Well, he does draw attention to himself in one small way – he campaigns for cleaner beaches and against the dumping of raw sewage. Ironic really, while most of his former comrades are still pumping it out.

Thrasybulus of Miletus

Thrasybulus was a tyrant on the Aegean island of Miletus in the seventh century BC. Everybody had tyrants in those days – there wasn't the stigma attached to the name that there is today ('he's a proper tyrant, he is') mainly because if you spoke out against them they'd kill you. Having said that, some of them had some pretty good ideas about statesmanship and keeping control of the population. Thrasybulus's mate Periander was also a tyrant, in Corinth on the Greek mainland (they must have met at a conference or something) and Periander once sent a messenger to Miletus to ask his friend about the best way to protect himself from being deposed. Thrasybulus took the messenger for a walk in a cornfield and knocked the heads off the tallest stalks by swiping them with his stick. The messenger went back to Periander who took the hint and busily went about bumping off all the most prominent citizens.

Now I'm not advocating judicial murder or political assassination as a way of running a country but I would say this tale is a good lesson for anyone who has ever thought of themselves as a stalk in a cornfield (basically everybody). We are all living in the cornfield and there is no shortage of tyrannical types in every walk of life ready to knock our heads off at the slightest excuse. Keeping your head down is the perfect advice in all situations – don't excel, don't speak up, don't show off, don't stand out.

Andrei Gromyko

The living embodiment of Thrasybulus's advice is the great Russian foreign minister of the 50s, 60s and 70s. He held his post for almost thirty years, having already outlasted Stalin, probably history's top murderer. He went on to survive the shoe-banging of Khrushchev, the all-enveloping eyebrows of Brezhnev, the not-doing-very-much of Andropov and the who-was-he-again? of Chernenko. When Gorbachev came in he was kicked upstairs and replaced by Eduard Shevardnadze – one of the greatest Scrabble hands in history.

You could argue that holding one of the most prominent positions in the Soviet Union for almost thirty years hardly counts as keeping one's head down, but remember from Stalin to Gorbachev anyone anywhere could wake up with an ice-pick in the head. So a lowly citizen stood as much chance of being bumped off as a top general.

How did Gromyko manage this feat? It seems by being as terse, grumpy and uncommunicative as possible. His nicknames were 'Comrade Nyet' and 'Grim Grom' and a story goes that he was coming out of a Washington hotel one morning when a reporter asked: 'Minister Gromyko, did you enjoy your breakfast today?'

He replied: 'Perhaps.'

This brilliantly understated hostility no doubt ensured he had very few friends. And since in politics most people are ultimately stabbed in the back by their friends, it seems like Mr Gromyko had it all worked out.

John Major

Another quiet, grey man who, as the saying goes, 'rose without trace'. John Major spent about ten years footling around in the lower reaches of the Conservative Party minding his own business, learning about banking and then, almost without being aware it was happening to him, became Foreign Secretary, Chancellor of the Exchequer and Prime Minister in the space of what seemed like a couple of weeks.

He stood in the abattoir of Thatcher's last government, while the bolt gun was aimed at Geoffrey Howe's and then Nigel

Lawson's head. Eventually when the mad cow herself was led off, he was the only creature left standing. He'd made it to the very top without doing anything at all about it.

Like the Emperor Claudius everyone around him probably thought John Major was a harmless nerd with a comedy-boring voice. This is a lesson we can all learn but it seems only reality TV contestants have picked this up – the people who go furthest in *Big Brother* and *The Apprentice* tend to be the boringly efficient; all show-offs and loudmouths are eliminated early because you'll always find enough people to hate them.

In the end becoming Prime Minister was John Major's big mistake because a boring PM becomes offensively dull: people tend to notice that kind of thing on the world stage. Also, having an affair with Edwina Currie, the brashest, most loudmouthed woman in Britain at the time, wasn't going to help him to remain inconspicuous, although to be fair to John Major, I don't think he was ever going to boast about it.

Books Every Boy Should Read

No matter how rubbish a book may be, if it's popular there will be a chorus of 'experts' saying – 'well at least it gets them reading'. What about comics? They get kids reading. The *Beano*, the *Dandy* and the *Topper* were my only reading matter until I was eleven. After that I got serious and started reading *Shoot!*

Many of the books on these 'approved' lists for boys happen to be the ones parents read when they were kids. Unfortunately, classics though they may be, there is nothing to stop a child from thinking they're rubbish. No one should feel they have failed in any sense because they or their kids don't think much of *Wind in the Willows*. It's not a crime to think Toad is an insufferable tosser and Mole is a big wuss. And is there anything worse than some parent you know telling you how much seven-year-old Nathaniel loves *Harry Potter* and has read all of them from cover to cover, by himself? Especially when your own children tell you they still prefer books which squeak when you press the cover. I do hate prescribed reading lists of any kind (unless you're studying for a degree or something) so feel free in joining me to slag this lot off...

Winnie the Pooh

A A Milne

The bear is irritating in the extreme, as are all the other psychiatric cases in that bloody Hundred Acre Wood. There's a donkey with depression, an overanxious piglet, a hyperactive tiger and the bear itself is an addict with ADHD.

Thomas the Tank Engine

Rev. Awdry

More characters with behavioural problems. Thomas and most of the engines are conceited egomaniacs, except Toby and Edward who at least have a degree of self-awareness. The railway is badly run with a terrible safety record.

The Secret Seven

Enid Blyton

90 per cent padding, 10 per cent story.

Most of it is just about some kids meeting up in a shed, eating biscuits and wondering what will happen this week. There's a knock at the door – who is it?

'It's Colin.'

'Come in, Colin.'

[Door knock]

'Is that Jack?'

'No, it's Barbara.'

'Come in.'

Etc., etc.

Harry Potter *and the ...*

(...seven books in total – way too long and pointless to mention here)

J K Rowling

Tom Brown's Schooldays with wizards and elves. A big plug for private education. The films might be better, but who cares?

The Thirty Nine Steps

John Buchan

The film is better (the Hitchcock version anyway) – at least it has a decent ending: 'Where are the thirty-nine steps?'

'The thirty-nine steps is a criminal organisation of spies...' BANG.

In the book they just find thirty-nine steps and arrest some baddies. That's it.

His Dark Materials

Philip Pullman

The film is better – oh, no, it isn't actually, it's shit.

The Lion the Witch and the Wardrobe

C S Lewis

Why the allegory? Isn't the New Testament good enough for you?

The Discworld series

Terry Pratchett

More elves and sorcery. If you want your child to have a nerdish interest in wargaming and heavy metal, read on. But be warned, the next and more alarming phase is ...

The Lord of the Rings Trilogy

J R R Tolkien

Each book is about a billion pages too long.

The Hitchhiker's Guide to the Galaxy*

Douglas Adams

More nerd-fodder. This time sci-fi. The answer is 42, ha ha! And the names are hilarious, aren't they? Zaphod Beeblebrox, Slartibartfast – genius!

*Not really a proper book as it began life as a radio series.

Non Essential Kit for Boys:

A Compass

'You can make your own compass with a bowl of water, a magnet, a cork and a needle.'

Brilliant. I assume we've found the cure for cancer then?

Apparently, a compass will always help a boy who's a bit lost, after a spiffing day full of adventure, to find his way safely home.

How does it do that?

'By pointing out where North is, of course.'

And what use is that without a map showing the points of the compass?

'Er ...'

So the adventurous boy not only has to carry a compass around, he needs a chart as well, preferably stored for safekeeping in a mahogany chest which he carts around with him all day in a wheelbarrow.

Without a map of the known world what is the good of knowing where any North, East or Sou-Sou'Westerly point is if you don't know where you're supposed to be heading? I've been alive for almost fifty years and in all that time I don't remember people discussing where they lived in cartographical terms or with reference to a compass. I never heard, in those supposedly halcyon days when kids were allowed to roam free over hill and dale, my parents ever telling me as I set off to play: 'Mark ye, we abide 36 degrees North East of Doncaster and keep ye the sun at thy back for the growing moss doth westward go.'

Also, I may be a complete dunderhead, but when you look at a compass and the needle is pointing at the 'W' for West, what are you supposed to do? Spin around until the needle is pointing at the 'N'? Spinning round isn't always the best way to orientate yourself. You'll be so busy staring at the compass needle you'll either walk into oncoming traffic or head-first into a tree.

No, knowing where North is has never helped, and certainly these days most people under the age of thirty have no idea whether Ipswich is north or south of Rochdale.

It's always been a mystery to me why childhood adventures and boyish larking about are supposed to be somehow incomplete without a compass.

Poetry

There's been a big campaign in the last year to inspire young people with a love of poetry. This is quite a tall order because, in comics and cartoons and the works of Nigel Molesworth, poetry equals cissy, big-girls' blouse and a weedy wet. The campaign has been mainly conducted on Radio 4 and BBC2 and tells you all you need to know about the middle-class anxiety over the state of Childhood today.

Years ago, the campaign argues, we all learned poems by heart – Keats, Wordsworth, chunks of Shakespeare, Alexander Pope, Alfred Tennyson – and loved it, apparently. These days though, children are not encouraged to learn or even read poetry and so they wander in a cultural desert, waiting for people like Griff Rhys Jones and Daisy Goodwin and James Naughtie and Jeremy Paxman to rescue them.

Now, I quite like poetry these days if I stumble across a forgotten one by accident, but the only verses I ever learned as a child were the ones I was forced to, for an exam. For various reasons the teachers on both my 'O' and 'A' level English course disappeared about five weeks before the exams. Fortunately our Deputy Head was a kind of academic Andy McNab, abseiling into the classroom in the nick of time to sort the trouble out. Basically he forced us to learn by rote as much of the set texts as possible. This was a bit difficult with *Tess of the d'Urbervilles* but huge speeches from *Measure for Measure* and *King Lear* and the whole of *The Wasteland* were committed to memory. As a remedial method of teaching it worked a treat and the necessary exams were negiotiated. But has it enriched me in any way? Alan Bennett, speaking through the rather fruity sixth-form teacher in *The History Boys,* argues that even though these poems mean nothing to us as children, we should learn them off by heart so that when we do reach the age when they might mean something to us, they will come back and console us. Well, that's a great argument for rote-learning but it's about as powerful to a young person as the piano-lesson lecture: 'You might hate it now but when you're older you'll wish you'd done your practice.' The operative words for a kid are 'hate it now'.

And when I think about it, is it really such a great consolation to me to have the words of T S Eliot wedged in my brain. 'Consider Phlebas who was once as handsome and as tall as you' – I'm stuck with that one but I can't say it's helped me through any dark nights of the soul. Or Shakespeare? 'Blow, winds, and crack your cheeks! Rage, blow, you cataracts and hurricanoes' – I'm stuck with that one, too. I have occasionally tossed it out during a spell of bad weather to the amazement of no one. Even the poems of Ted Hughes and his woody woody woodpeck pecky pecky bird bark binding book of bollocks are safely lodged in the brain bank, and all I can say is, no wonder Sylvia Plath topped herself.

There appears to be an approved list of poems, in certain books that make it their business to prescribe reading matter for children, which young people are supposed to know off by heart.

Below are the responses to seven poems, that I would imagine a ten-year-old boy would give upon being instructed to learn them purely because someone told him 'That's what *I* had to do.'

Useful Knowledge

If by Rudyard Kipling

> *'If you can keep your head when all about you are losing theirs and blaming it on you ...'*

What?! Why are they blaming me? I ain't done nuffink ...

Ozymandias by Percy Bysshe Shelley

> *'I met a traveller from an antique land who said: two vast and trunkless legs of stone stand in the desert ...'*

Yeah whatever.

Song of Myself by Walt Whitman

> *'I, now, thirty-seven years old in perfect health begin ...'*

Thirty-seven? You are *soooo* old!

Vitae Lampada by Sir Henry Newbolt

> *'There's a breathless hush in the Close tonight ...'*

Yeah, *X Factor*'s on, innit brilliant?

Sea-Fever by John Masefield

> *'I must go down to the seas again, to the vagrant gypsy life ...'*

Ha Ha, Pikeys!

Rime of the Ancient Mariner by Samuel Taylor Coleridge

> *'It is an Ancient Mariner,*
> *And he stoppeth one of three ...'*

Grimsby Town need a new 'keeper.

The Tyger by William Blake

> *'Tyger! Tyger! burning bright,*
> *In the forests of the night ...'*

You've spelt tiger wrong.

Punctuation

Going around openly correcting people's punctuation is not a public service; it's not a brave thing to do, it's just stupid. It's asking for a smack in the mouth just as much as challenging someone who has dropped a crisp packet in the street to pick it up.

I used to be a stickler for punctuation until I read *Eats, Shoots And Leaves*, the *Mein Kampf* for humourless pedants everywhere. It used to matter to me that people know how to use a semicolon properly; even if I don't. I used to scoff at people who put the apostrophe in the wrong place – like greengrocer's and pub landlord's. And then I read Lynn Trus's's' book and it felt like that *Mitchell and Webb* sketch where two German soldiers realise, from the skull and crossbones on their uniform, that they are the baddies. I'd go even further and say that punctuation in the hands of the sticklers and the pedants is like the Cross of St George in the hands of the British National Party. It's turned something that represented decency and civilisation into something to be feared and shunned. So, I want nothing to do with the rules of punctuation any more. It's a way of looking down and sneering at people – probably far more young and working-class people use punctuation properly than don't.

The howl of anguish over the demise of 'proper punctuation' is, of course, another form of childhood nostalgia, just like people banging on about why children don't use pea-shooters any more. Lynn Truss herself describes her feelings about a misplaced apostrophe as a 'ghastly private emotional process similar to the stages of bereavement'. But most stages of bereavement don't demand that everyone else in the world feels as bad about it as you do. The punctuation pedants want everyone to be outraged on their behalf, like those people who send letters to the *Daily Telegraph* such as: 'Whatever happened to red tomatoes?' or 'Why do people insist on saying train when they mean locomotive?' or 'Am I the only person in the country to notice the demise of the real pie?'

Lynn Truss actually encourages her readers – whom she would clearly love to be officially incorporated into a kind of Semicolon Stasi – to sneak up to greengrocers' stalls and place her apostrophe stickers (they came free with the paperback edition) in the correct place on the Fresh Lettuce's and Ripe Banana's and other offensive listings. I hope you'll join me in encouraging the nation's greengrocers to get as many stickers as they can from their apples and melons and stick them all over copies of Lynn Truss's' book.

● ● ● ● ● ● ● ● ● ● ● ● ● ●

Grammar

● ●

This is just as worrying as punctuation and the angry cries for a return to strict lessons in English sentence construction for all children echo around the same newspaper columns as do the calls to bring back hanging.

It's hard to resist the temptation to have all people who say, 'I would of' instead of 'I would have' thrown into a tiger's cage, but some of the things grammarian Nazis get worked up about are really quite harmless. The 'fewer' or 'less' blunder is the one that really revolts the pedants and will actually provoke them into correcting you to your face. Apparently, '10 items or less' is wrong, it should be '10 items or fewer', but how stupid does that sound? You know what? I really couldn't care fewer if it happens less times or not.

There are some kind souls who try to write people-friendly books about grammar (must check those sales figures) and who want to *encourage* us to be better at grammar and spelling rather than threaten us with Lynne Truss-style humiliation, so they are always generating well-meaning but rather pointless mnemonics to help us. E.g. (or i.e. if you want to piss someone off):

I before E except after C

... and except when it's in the words – weird, neighbour, poltergeist, being, seize, kaleidoscope, vein, feisty, sovereignty . . . this isn't very useful, is it?

When two vowels go walking the first does the talking
e.g. 'oat' or 'eat'

Oh, really – what about 'shoe', 'bear' and 'feint'?

Big Elephants Can Always Understand Small Elephants.

It's only seven letters for God's sake! How hard is it to forget?

Believe has a lie in the middle

Who are you, Dan Brown?

Once there was a young woman named Sep. She was violently afraid of rodents, especially rats. One day, her little brother, who was a very cruel, unfeeling child, tapped her shoulder, and yelled 'Sep, a rat!' Her response, of course, was a loud 'Eeeeeee!'

This little ditty is supposed to help you remember how to spell 'separate'. I honestly think I'd be able to memorise half the dictionary before I could remember that. Utter rubbish.

Non Essential Kit for Boys:
A Large Marble

A Taw is the big marble you shoot to knock the other ones out of the 'otty', or whatever you call the circle around the marbles in your part of the world. I actually loved playing 'mabs' and I loved looking at the elaborate, multicoloured ones that no one ever seemed to buy in shops but won in competition.

What I don't understand is why you'd want to carry one around with you at all times. This would be asking for trouble, in the shape of a bigger kid from another school who would tweak your ear or give you Chinese burns until you surrendered it to him.

These bigger kids tended to favour steel ball-bearings as their shooting marble, or 'bollies' as they used to call them at my school. Most of these bollies were stolen from the pit where they probably once helped various scary types of coal-cutting machinery to run smoothly. The appeal for the violent, bullying type of kid who owned a bolly was that it could do untold damage to people and property if fired from an industrial-strength catapult, of the sort used by professional rat-catchers in the olden days. Don't you think that the deeper you delve into nostalgia the more depressing it sounds?

So there's nothing really terribly wrong with marbles apart from the occasional problem they can cause for bored children. I'm sure we've all done it – you've been playing mabs for half an hour, got a bit bored, so you stuff one up your nostril or into your earhole and spend the rest of the day in casualty. Or, because it was the 1960s when I did it, the next week in casualty.

The Tyranny of Excellence

We want the best for our kids, right? We want them to have what we didn't. Our parents struggled so that we could step up just one rung on the ladder above them. But that appears not to be enough today. We not only want our kids to have more than we did, we want them to have more than anyone else's. We want them to have more language skills, more musical, theatrical, academic accomplishments than anyone; we want them to obliterate the opposition. We brief them and train them and equip them, not for a normal life, but as if they were being dropped behind enemy lines with Clint Eastwood and Richard Burton. But as many a thriller like *Where Eagles Dare* will tell you, too much knowledge is a dangerous thing. ('Now that you know my plans, I'm afraid I will have to kill you.')

Why this obsession with excellence? 'Be the best, accept nothing less!'. I don't want to be pernickety (OK, I do; it's fun), but strictly speaking, only one person can have the best. Everyone else has to make do with sloppy seconds. In striving for 'The Best' you bring nothing but pain, anger, bitterness, jealousy, disappointment, frustration and resentment. As I have said in many places through-out this book, the best you should hope for is mediocrity. Only aspire to the slightly above-average. No one will resent you, no one will take pot-shots at you, no one will try to bully you out of your average-ness (except maybe a pushy parent). No one will be disappointed when you don't live up to expectations.

Useful Knowledge

Why not just take it easy? By being only slightly above average you will be more at ease with the world. No one expects you to be brilliant – if you happen to do something quite well once in a blue moon, well that's a bonus. But don't ever be brilliant. John Cleese is only ever a let-down these days – no one forgives him for not being quite as good as he was in *Fawlty Towers*. What happened to Michael Owen since that goal against Argentina in 1998? And if you're looking for the ultimate example of unfulfilled promise, look no further than Go West. Everyone waited for a follow-up single to come close to the magic of 'We Close Our Eyes', but we waited in vain.

Many parents – middle class, comfortably off and anxious to achieve The Best – don't want their kids being dragged down or held back by thickos or oiks or hooligans. So they pay big money to relocate them to a bizarre world where, apparently, every skill can be acquired, every fact can be known, every instrument mastered and 'The Best' is quite definitely achievable. Obviously the big investment is private school, and many people justify that by saying they just want the education they had for free in the Good Old Days, and the only way to get that now is to pay for it. Some private schools think the way to achieve this is to lock kids in a classroom for eight hours a day and force-feed them KNOWLEDGE like foie gras geese.

This is, in essence, the whole problem with the current wave of nostalgia for a golden age of childhood. In the past, apparently, we just absorbed poetry, mathematics, botany, biology, history and science as we skipped through the fields on endless sunny afternoons, picking up frogs and beetles and singing verses from Dante's *Inferno*. Now, as adults we feel we have to expend huge amounts of money and time on recreating these ideal conditions which we force our children to endure. And even when the school day is done, there's more, as we enrol our children in a range of completely inappropriate over-priced training schemes, boot camps and hoop-jumping exercises that destroy the very childhood we are trying to salvage.

Bibliography

The Dangerous Book for Boys
The Boys' Book: How to be the Best at Everything
The Boys' Book 2: How to Be the Best at Everything Again
The Boys' Annual
211 Things a Bright Boy Can Do
The Pocket Dangerous Book for Boys: Things to Do
The Dangerous Book for Boys Yearbook
The Pocket Dangerous Book for Boys: Things to Know
The Dads' Book for the Dad Who's Best at Everything
The Dangerous Book of Heroes
The Pocket Dangerous Book for Boys: Facts, Figures and Fun
The Boys' Book of Spycraft
Things to do with Dad
The Family Book: Amazing Things To Do Together
The Grandads' Book: For the Grandad Who's Best at Everything
Dad Manual: How to Be a Brilliant Father
Dad Stuff: Shedloads of Ideas for Dads
For Boys Only: The Biggest Baddest Book Ever
The Big Book of Boys Stuff
The Curious Boys Book of Exploration
The Curious Boys Book of Adventure
The Boys Book of Survival
The Boys Book of Outdoor Survival
The Boys Book of Backyard Camping
The Pocket Guide To Boy Stuff

The Mammoth Book of Boys Own Stuff
The Outdoor Book for Adventurous Boys
The Adventurous Book of Outdoor Games: Classic Fun for Daring Boys and Girls.
The Blessing of a Skinned Knee
The Dads Book of Exposing Infants on a Mountainside
Rip Your Guts Out On A Barbed Wire Fence Like We Used To Do When We Were Kids
The Dad's Book of Lads' Best Mate's Child's Uncle's Top Toy Tips
The Mum's Book of Boys Things To Give Dad To Do With Lads
The Grandad's Book of Mum's Favourite Respectable Mentor's Proper Fun Wizard Pranks With Pater
Back When I Was A Lad, All We Did Was Whittle
Isn't Wood Brilliant?
Your Kids Play Computer Games? Call Yourself A Father?
Why Can't Things Be Like They Used To?
Dad's Stuff for Stuffy Dads
The Boys Book of Buses and Trains
The Boys Book of Home-made Weaponry
The Boys Book of Nazi Regalia
The Dangerous Book of Not Really Very Dangerous Things

*Some of these are made up, but can you guess which?

Acknowledgements

Thanks to editor Malcolm Croft, agent Jennifer Christie, and to Stephanie, James and Mikey for their encouragement. Also thanks to Wikipedia for helping lazy people make a living.

"I'd like to say that this is a funny, intelligent, thorough account of not bothering to expand your horizons, but I can't be arsed."
Paul Merton

Here's a fact: there are at least 100 books out there that tell you the various things you should do before you die. (There may be more but we couldn't be arsed to count them.) 'Swim with dolphins!' – they squeal. Jump out of a plane from a great height! Read Kafka in Prague! Have a meaningful conversation with a beggar! (Yes, really.)

But will these things actually make our lives more meaningful?

For those who are looking for an escape-route; a guilt-free reason NOT to spend their hard-earned cash on deli-belly in India, or broken limbs on the ski slopes of the Alps, *Can't Be Arsed* shows the other side of the coin. It hilariously exposes the harsh reality of these so-called 'adventures', giving you the perfect excuse to stay at home and crack open a beer on the sofa.

£9.99 • Hardback • 9781906032371